# CONSTABLE AROUND THE VILLAGE

A perfect feel-good read from one of Britain's best-loved authors

*Constable Nick Mystery Book 3*

## NICHOLAS RHEA

JOFFE
BOOKS

Revised edition 2020
Joffe Books, London
www.joffebooks.com

Cover credit: Colin Williamson
www.colinwilliamsonprints.com

ISBN: 978-1-78931-370-3

# CHAPTER ONE

Ill customs influence my very senses.
SIR GEORGE ETHEREGE, 1635—1691

Somewhere across the map of North Yorkshire there lies an invisible line which separates the north of that county from the south. People in counties Durham and Cleveland will accept a north North Yorkshireman as a northerner, but those unfortunates who live in the southern regions of North Yorkshire, in the soft warmth and built-up wilderness of cities like York and Ripon and boroughs like Scarborough and Harrogate, are considered southerners.

In every northerner's eyes, a southerner is suspect. There is something not quite right about them. If that southerner happens to qualify only because he lives in the southern part of North Yorkshire, then that makes no difference. Anyone unenlightened enough to live south of that unseen line is indeed a person to be pitied, more so if he happens to live in a town. *Pity* is perhaps not the right word; *tolerance* is not totally apt and neither is *deplore*. A feeling of despair may not be absolutely accurate, nor is excruciation, agony, passion, or anxiety.

If there is difficulty in finding a word suitable to describe that feeling, the north North Yorkshireman will come to the

1

rescue by saying, "Ah can't abide southerners." Having said that, he knows what he means. He can't abide them; there's a lot that a Yorkshireman can't abide, but, as a group, southerners are definitely the least abideable of anyone.

The snag is that the all-important, but invisible line is very difficult to define or determine. No one is quite sure where it lies, least of all the self-appointed northerners.

In my capacity as the village constable at Aidensfield, I lived somewhere on that line. I appreciated that fact when I was posted there; having been reared *in a genuine* northern district, the moorlands of the North Riding of Yorkshire, I had been brought up in the knowledge that the area around Aidensfield was definitely "south". Even though the outer limits of Aidensfield beat encompassed the southern edges of the North Yorkshire moors and lay well within the North Riding's administrative area, the village was definitely "south" in the eyes of many.

Once I moved into Aidensfield, however, I did not consider it "south". In my view, it was north because the folks who lived there spoke the same language as my ancestors and adopted the same hard-headed attitude. In fact, the villagers considered themselves "north"; in their view, southerners lived at York or beyond and occupied those indeterminable areas of suburbia between there and London, which was a biggish town located at the bottom end of the Great North Road.

Having been nurtured as a northerner, finding myself working in what they consider a southern district was disconcerting. Even so, I was confident that Aidensfield really was "north". But who could decide the issue? There had to be some definitive method of settling the matter. Somewhere, somehow, there had to be a rule which clearly and permanently categorised North Yorkshiremen. Perhaps a road, a river or a parish boundary or two? By chance I stumbled upon the answer. It lay in the ancient custom of First Footing, a matter in which I, as the local constable, soon found myself deeply involved.

First Footing of the genuine kind does not take place in the south. That is a golden rule. Worse still, in some southern areas the people attempt to copy the custom by doing it on Christmas Day! That is sheer impudence. First Footing is purely a northern custom and, because the villagers of Aidensfield and district take part in the custom, they must be northerners. In those days the people of York didn't genuinely First Foot while those in the West Riding, at centres like Leeds and Bradford, certainly did not. Further away in the deep, deep south of Yorkshire, at Sheffield, (which is halfway to London), the matter was not even considered. Down there, they thought First Footing was a building term. But Aidensfield did First Foot. That classified it as north and that made me happy. It meant I had not trespassed beyond the bounds of true northern credibility by emigrating into unknown southern regions and, even if my old colleagues continued to categorise Aidensfield as south, I knew it wasn't. That the custom of First Footing occurred in Aidensfield assured me it was a northern village and for that I was eternally thankful. For a northerner to be mistaken for a southerner was akin to a Catholic being mistaken for a Holy Roller.

First Footing is a very ancient and noble custom. It is practised with alacrity on New Year's Eve and its misty origins matter very little to those who enjoy it in our modern society. Nonetheless, there are certain rules which must be obeyed.

First and foremost, it is a New Year ceremony, the purpose of which is to bring good luck and prosperity to the household. The method of First Footing is very simple, albeit undertaken within the accepted but unwritten code of conduct.

The term means "first into the house". A First Foot is therefore the very first visitor to a house in the New Year. He must arrive as soon as possible after midnight on New Year's morning and he must bring with him certain gifts which symbolise a lasting supply of food, warmth and prosperity.

These items are fairly simple — there must be a piece of coal to symbolise heat and light, a coin to symbolise continuing wealth or perhaps a little salt in lieu, and a piece of bread to fulfil the food requirement. In Aidensfield and some other areas of North Yorkshire, a piece of holly must also be carried, this evergreen being an ancient symbol of everlasting life.

In addition to the required gifts, the First Foot must also comply with certain personal rules. He must always be a man. Women must never perform this task, otherwise it brings bad luck, and the Sex Discrimination Act has not yet been amended to change this rule. In order to qualify, a man must never be flat-footed or cross-eyed, and his eyebrows must not meet across the nose. In addition, he should have dark hair. In the ideal situation, he should be a total stranger who chances to enter one's house at the right time, but, as honest midnight visitors of this sex are rare and indeed open to close police interest, most northerners make do with someone they know, provided he is suitably qualified.

To ensure that each household is visited at the necessary time, plans are made well in advance. The selected First Footer is approached and asked if he will execute this noblest of deeds for the everlasting benefit of the household in question. Invariably, he says he will be happy to oblige. Thus committed, he must equip himself with sufficient bread, money or salt, coal and holly, for each house upon his itinerary and he will be expected to kiss every lady encountered *en route*.

The selection of a suitable First Footer, or Lucky Bird as he is often known, is therefore a matter of some importance. Tall, dark men are in demand as careful plans are laid. As zero hour approaches, the doors are locked until the arrival of the First Foot. It would be disastrous if someone else entered to ruin the luck of the coming year.

It ought to be said at this stage that there is another seasonal custom in the north. This also takes place over New Year's Eve and well into the early hours of New Year's Day, and it is known as Boozing Late. All the pubs and clubs work hard to cater for massive thirsts and seasonal celebrations and it is fair to say that a high proportion of the indigenous population inhabit these places as the Old Year changes into the New. Much singing and high-spirited jollification takes place and a great deal of last-minute First Footing is arranged at these celebratory gatherings.

It follows, therefore, that the role of the country constable is somewhat unspecific over those midnight hours. The pubs make brave attempts to comply with the law by seeking permission from Their Worships to open late. This is seldom refused, if only because Their Worships also enjoy the occasion, and the customers play their part by never drinking away from their home village at New Year. Thus they are all "friends of the licensee" which means they drink later than normal and this also obviates the constable's worries about drunks navigating ungovernable vehicles about the place. Everyone walks, or tries to. Another feature of this arrangement is that, by walking, one can call at many houses *en route,* ostensibly to check that the First Foot has performed his annual ritual. If he hasn't, entry is refused; if he has, everyone is welcome to take cheese and gingerbread, laced with ginger wine.

On my very first New Year's Eve at Aidensfield, therefore, I found myself on duty and having to perform half nights. It was a shift beginning at 6 pm on New Year's Eve and ending at 2 am on New Year's Day. This fact registered itself with horror on my mind, but as the newest newcomer to Ashfordly section it was my lot to be allocated this duty. It meant I would have to patrol my beat for eight miserable hours while everyone else was welcoming the New Year in the traditional northern manner.

The pubs would be full of merry-making and the houses noisy with parties. The streets would be deserted, at least for the final throes of the Old Year. My role would be to enforce the law that night, to patrol my wide-ranging beat on a cold, noisy motorcycle and to return home in the early hours of

New Year's Day frozen to the core and reeling at the absence of pure enjoyment. It threatened to be a miserable time.

But the general public had other ideas. Because I was almost six feet tall with dark hair and eyebrows that did not meet in the middle, plus the fact that I was, in truth, a stranger to the district and a person of the male sex to boot, I was deemed eminently suited for the role of a First Footer. Little did I realise, as I embarked on my evening patrol shortly after six o'clock, that my New Year's Eve would be both memorable and enjoyable.

As I began that final Old Year tour of duty, I made a mental note to First Foot at my own house on New Year's Day. I would be my own First Footer at two o'clock that morning. If all else failed, I would achieve that honour. But as I chugged into Aidensfield, parked my motorcycle and embarked upon a foot patrol to the pillar-box a lady hailed me.

She was middle-aged with greying hair and wore a flowered apron about her ample body. It transpired she had spotted me marching past her tiny cottage and had rushed to the door to call me. In the blackness of that early evening, I must have looked horrifying in my crash-helmet, goggles and motorcycle gear, but it did not frustrate this determined woman.

"Mr Rhea, Mr Rhea," she called. "Have you a moment?"

I halted, turned and beamed at her from beneath my heavy clothing.

"Hello, Mrs Mitchell."

"I'm glad I caught you." She was panting slightly. "I wonder if I might ask you a favour?"

"Go ahead," I invited, wondering what lay in store.

"Tonight," she smiled. "It's New Year's Eve and I haven't a First Footer."

"Do you want me to find one?" I asked, innocently.

"Well, no, not exactly." She didn't lose her smile. "I thought you might do it for me."

"Oh." I must have sounded surprised, then realised I was being paid a compliment. "Well, yes, I will. I'm sure I can manage that."

"At midnight," she told me. "You must come at midnight, or as soon as you can afterwards."

"Let me see." I made a mental calculation of the conference points I had to make. I had one at eleven-thirty at Elsinby and my next was twelve-fifteen at Aidensfield.

"Yes, I can be there," I offered. "I'll do your First Footing."

"You'll need a piece of coal, some holly, money and bread," she said seriously. "I'll get them for you."

And with no more ado Mrs Mitchell returned to her home and moments later reappeared with the necessary items. I opened one of the panniers on the motorcycle and popped in the coal and holly. I slid the £.s.d. penny and slice of bread into my overcoat pocket.

"Midnight," she said, "not before."

"I'll be there," I assured her.

Having settled that little issue, I completed my journey to the pillar-box, popped in a birthday card I had to post and began the return trip to my motorcycle. As I did so, I reflected briefly on the honour she had bestowed upon me. I felt this request had come to me because of my comparatively recent arrival in the village, but at the same time it showed that I was accepted. It proved I was allowed into the homes of the people otherwise than in the course of my duty. I was part of the life of the community. That's how I interpreted this request and it pleased me.

Within the next three hours, I was approached by seven further villagers, all wanting me to be their First Footer. I was given lumps of coal which filled one pannier while sprigs of holly were pushed unceremoniously into the other. I had a coat pocket full of sliced bread wrapped in greaseproof paper and lots of coins jangling about my uniform. The situation had now arrived whereby I had to make notes about the precise timing of my First Footing activities.

Mrs Mitchell could be accommodated just after midnight, for I would then have returned from Elsinby in readiness for my twelve-fifteen point at Aidensfield telephone kiosk. This was no problem. I had also to remember that

Sergeant Blaketon was on duty tonight and he was quite likely to pay me a call, so I didn't dare miss any of my rendezvous points. So it was to be Mrs Mitchell at midnight, Stan Williams at ten past, my point at quarter past, Mr and Mrs Collins at twenty-five past, Mrs Collins's mother next door at half past, the elderly Misses Bush and Rowe at quarter to one, Alan and Sue Bentley at one o'clock and the Leech family at quarter past one. I would make my one-thirty point at Thackerston and that would get me home at two o'clock, there to perform my final and most important First Foot duty. My night of threatened misery had taken a turn for the better and time would fly.

It seemed a reasonable night's work. From eight o'clock until nine, therefore, I patrolled the beat with holly sticking from one pannier and a fair tonnage of coal in the other, ending my first half of the tour at home for supper. I tucked into a warm pie before the fire and laughed with Mary as I explained my forthcoming "duties". The children were tucked snugly in bed and Mary said she would go upstairs when I left home at quarter to ten.

It would be a lonely New Year for her, but with the children so tiny it was impossible to go out and baby-sitters were difficult to acquire on such an evening. Stoically, Mary accepted her domesticity and I kissed her farewell as I began the second and most arduous part of my tour of duty.

As there had been no sign of Sergeant Blaketon and no other official calls upon my time, I decided to pay an early visit to all the pubs on my patch. Sight of the uniform would remind the revellers of the presence of the law and that alone should cause most of the merry-makers to enjoy themselves within reasonable limits and to refrain from punch-ups and wild drunkenness.

I discovered that at every pub there was a party. As each had been granted an extension of hours, every bar, lounge, hall and passage was full to overflowing, with many of the landlords putting free food at the disposal of the customers. In addition, there was a stock of streamers, balloons, funny hats and kissable young ladies; even at this early hour, a good time was assured.

Cars and motorcycles were noticeably absent; I was pleased to note the basic common sense of the merry-makers and mentally praised them for leaving such liabilities at home. In every case, the pub atmosphere was superb. Every building radiated happiness and *bonhomie* as its inmates worked towards the explosive climax that was twelve midnight. That would be the signal for everyone to kiss everyone else, for the champagne to flow, for First Footers to roam the streets and for all kinds of resolutions to be made. It would be a time of joy and fun.

Outside those doors, it was a different world. The bucolic lanes were silent. No one moved between these isolated centres of population. Everyone was at home, waiting for midnight. There was no moon and the countryside lay dormant with just a hint of frost. The only moving thing was my motorcycle with me astride it. I began to ponder upon the value of this presence. Eleven o'clock came and went without incident. Other than the controlled revelry in the pubs, the countryside was at its most peaceful and serene. Houses with lights at the windows dotted the remote parts showing there was life beyond the pubs and, for five minutes, I sat astride the machine at the top of Aidensfield Bank and looked across the landscape spread below me. I felt no part of tonight's excitement. I felt as if I was a total outsider. I thought about the excitements, the friendships, the fellowship, the happiness and even the unsung misery being played out in the villages down there. From my hilltop vantage-point, I could see nothing but a carpet of darkness dotted here and there with pinpricks of light. Those lights however, represented happiness, distant lights with friendship behind them. And I was alone on my hilltop.

It's a miserable job being a policeman on such occasions. I knew I could not join the people in their merry-making because my uniform would immediately freeze any atmosphere of pleasure. I had to patrol alone. And so I did. I kicked the bike into life and moved off.

Occasionally I parked and walked the streets of peaceful villages in order to increase the circulation of my blood. It kept my fingers and toes warm and I made my allotted points at selected telephone kiosks. Surprisingly, the time passed quickly. It would soon be New Year.

After my eleven-thirty point at Elsinby, I paid a quick visit to the Hopbind Inn. I caught George's eye and waved at him across a sea of pink faces and hovering glasses. He beckoned me to the counter in the passage, leaned across and said in true landlord's style:

"Have one with us, Mr Rhea?"

I pondered. I did not normally drink on duty, but on this occasion he recognised my hesitancy and pressed home his advantage.

"Just a quickie. Small whisky? To see the New Year in?"

I looked at my watch. There was twenty minutes before Mrs Mitchell and my First Footing obligation. There was no sergeant about. I was cold and lonely . . .

"Aye, all right, George. For Auld Lang Syne."

He invited me into the packed bar but I tactfully declined, and he drew me a measure of finest malt whisky. In the passage, I raised the glass, toasted him and his customers and wished them all the happiness of the New Year, now only eighteen minutes away.

"Thanks, George," I returned the glass. "I appreciate that. Now I must dash—I'm First Footing at midnight."

"All in the course of duty!" he laughed and returned to his generous hosting.

The whisky had warmed me nicely and I felt the beginnings of a glow of happiness as I guided my little machine through the dark, deserted lanes. As I glided into Aidensfield, I could hear singing in the pub. All its lights were aglow as I parked the machine against the wall of the village hall. Like everyone else, I was in my home village for New Year. I checked my watch. It was two minutes to twelve. I waited. I knew I must not enter Mrs Mitchell's house before midnight, as that would bring bad luck. It was a long wait.

Finally, the church clock began to chime. Its long, measured tones brought the anxiously awaited news and the pub erupted into a cacophonous din. Trumpets blew, bagpipes wailed, voices were raised in song and a badly-tuned piano began to pick out the notes of Auld Lang Syne. Inside, it must have sounded heavenly. Outside, the racket was appalling. I waited and listened, feeling very, very miserable and very, very lonely. Then the door burst open and two men rushed out, each wearing a paper hat and carrying a balloon. At exactly the same time, both noticed me. I was about to move towards Mrs Mitchell's house but was too late.

"It's t'bobby!" I heard one of them splutter in slurred language and with some effort. "He'll do it . . . You ask him . . ."

"Yessh . . . good idea, John . . . very, very good idea . . . you asshk him."

Brave with drink, the two men came towards me, both evidently about to ask me something serious.

"Misshter Conshtable," said one of them. "Your presshensh issh required insshide, immediately if not sshooner," and he giggled at his little joke. "Now, immediately," and he saluted.

"Trouble?" I asked.

"No trouble, offissher, just Firsht Footing. There'ssh no one who can Firssht Foot, you sshee, because they're all in there now. It mussht be a stranger."

"All right, all right," I said.

"Great, great," and in they ran. I broke a little piece of holly from the adequate supply in my pannier, broke a piece of coal to gain the necessary lump, tore off a corner of bread and found a penny of my own.

Thus armed, I sallied into the smoky, alcoholic and happy atmosphere of the Brewers Arms. A huge shout of welcome erupted as my uniform materialised through the haze and I was manhandled through the crowd, being kissed by countless women until I reached the fireplace. There I knew I must deposit the coal, bread, money and holly. Surprisingly, the entire place fell silent. There was not a word as I made an exaggerated action to perform the necessary First Footing act and straightened up to find a huge glass of whisky before me. To have refused would have been churlish.

Cheers erupted about my ears as I brought guaranteed good luck to the Brewers Arms for the coming year and I raised my glass to wish happiness to everyone. The job over, the singing resumed, the kissing continued and the music commenced to the accompaniment of much back-slapping and hand-shaking as I quickly consumed the fiery contents of the glass.

Refusing another whisky on the grounds that I had an urgent appointment, I left the pub to make my way towards Mrs Mitchell's little house. It was now ten past twelve. I was ten minutes late and I found that my head was noticeably light and my walking action somewhat erratic. I had drunk the whisky far too quickly and the cool night air was causing me to amble from side to side. Nevertheless, I collected the necessary goods from my panniers and reached the cottage.

I knocked.

"Come in," she called from inside.

"It's P.C. Rhea," I opened the door and announced myself in case she thought it was a burglar.

Holding the coal, holly and slice of bread before me, I walked into her cosy living-room and swayed ever so slightly across the rug. Carefully, I placed one hand on the mantelshelf to steady myself and even more carefully placed the coal, holly and bread in the hearth, followed by the coin. My head was swimming slightly, but I was able to stand upright and wish her "Happy New Year".

"And a Happy New Year to you, Mr Rhea," she beamed. I had done well. The silence before this exchange was part of the ritual. It has been deemed that as the First Foot enters with his traditional gifts everyone must remain silent until he has deposited them in the hearth. Only then can the silence be broken.

"I have your drink ready," and she passed a glass of sherry to me.

I hadn't bargained for this. When accepting all these commitments, I thought my duties were merely to enter with the gifts and break in the New Year, but at every house I was expected to join the compulsory toast. I didn't dare refuse in case my lack of courtesy brought bad luck to everyone.

I gulped Mrs Mitchell's sherry because my point time was due and, after making something approximating an apology to her for my hurry, I rushed out to stand swaying near the telephone kiosk. My face was warm now and my entire body was responding to the liquor. Inside that hot motorcycle gear I was sweating profusely and decided that New Year duty wasn't too bad after all, even on half nights. No one rang me. Sergeant Blaketon did not make an appearance to wish me a Happy New Year and so I was left with the honourable duty of fulfilling all my other First Footing appointments.

At this stage, it was difficult to remember anything after Mrs Mitchell's sherry. I know that I did call upon all my other customers and a good many more besides. People kept pushing lumps of coal, sprigs of holly and slices of bread into my hands and I must have visited almost every house in Aidensfield, plonking coal, bread and holly into their hearths and downing indescribable concoctions as I offered slurred toasts to all and sundry. It must have been a happy time.

Instinctively, I knew I was in no fit state to ride the motorcycle back to my house and somehow, during the festivities, it got forgotten. The passage of time was also forgotten. I had no idea what the time was and became aware only of other demands for me to First Foot. It seemed that the entire population of the Brewers Arms took me into their homes to bring them luck.

After it all, I made my slow, laborious and hiccuping way back up the hill to the police house. I managed to fit my key into the lock and staggered inside, sweating and panting. I wiped my brow and my feet but recalled sufficient about my responsibilities to go into the living-room and place the coal, bread, coin and holly in the hearth. I must have remembered to bring these from my panniers, but as I stooped and swayed above my own fireside I noticed my hearth already contained those objects.

They weren't mine. Someone else had been. I had been surreptitiously First Footed! My gifts were still in my hands, all black with coal-dust and cold after the night's excesses. I stood for some minutes, wobbling before the sight in the hearth. Some unknown person had First Footed in *my* house. While I had been diligently patrolling, solving major crimes and protecting the public, someone had crept into my home and First Footed. Who? How? It was all too complicated for my fuddled brain and I simply placed my gifts beside the others, turned and struggled upstairs.

Memories of that awful ascent are hazy to say the least, the stairs presenting an almost insurmountable obstacle to my progress. I can recollect opening the bedroom door as quietly as possible before tripping over a chair and crashing unceremoniously onto the bed. Mary said something about it being a Happy New Year and I fell asleep, fully clothed, on top of the coverlet.

Next morning I was in severe trouble. My coal-black hands and motorcycle clothing had smeared the bed-clothes, the staircase, the walls and the living-room, to say nothing of the bathroom which had received me on occasions during those night hours. It looked as if a sweep had rampaged through the house. To make things worse, Sergeant Blaketon had come to the house at 2 am, expecting to find me booking off duty. On failing to find me, and thinking I had dodged in home early, he'd knocked on the door and had roused Mary and the children. He had then tried to overcome his error performing our First Footing, pinching my coal and breaking a twig off the holly-bush near the gate. From evidence thus acquired, it seems I had returned to base around 4 am, but I can't remember much about it.

On the credit side, my efforts did bring luck to the villagers. Later that year, Aidensfield Parish Council presented them with a street lamp.

\* \* \*

If my start to the year did not please Mary and the sergeant, it did please the village. From being a comparative stranger, I was now accepted as a villager, albeit with further reservations. I knew that I was regarded as a local person. My efforts at First Footing had ensured that, but I still had to prove myself as a policeman in the old-fashioned sense of the word. There's a big difference between a "person" and a "policeman" and my next task was to firmly establish myself in my official capacity.

This is more difficult than it seems. For one thing, it is never easy for a policeman to prove himself in the eyes of other policemen. To achieve that rare distinction, he must have an infinite capacity for arresting villains, drinking copious quantities of ale, dealing with "hard" men and sorting out problems of every kind. Proving oneself as a policeman in the eyes of the *public* is a totally different matter.

Members of the public view policemen in a particular light. They view them firstly as people and secondly as law-enforcement officers. I was sure that my status in the village as a person had been deemed satisfactory — my first few months had helped establish me in that sense, with my wife and young children helping enormously to make vital contacts. I had sealed that side of the business with my First Footing. But how could I prove myself a truly capable rural bobby in the eyes of the great British public? I required an important event, a big issue or emergency of some kind.

I waited for a suitable opportunity. It might be a crime to solve or a major incident to cope with. There might be a tough villain to conquer or a rescue operation of some kind. As the weeks went by, nothing happened. No crimes were committed, no villains fought me and no damsels required my rescue expertise.

As I patrolled my beautiful beat, alternating between the motorcycle and my own size nines, I remained vigilant as I anticipated the right opportunity. It almost became an obsession. I knew I had to show that I could be a policeman, as well as a person. But how? Nothing dramatic seemed to happen. No one got murdered or raped, no one had his house broken into or his car stolen, no one got lost on the moors or attacked in the street. Life was so unpleasantly peaceful. The sergeant grumbled because I didn't submit offence reports and the inspector nattered because I had recorded no arrests.

It was during one of my low spells, when I wanted drama to enter my mundane life, that I sensed a dramatic occurrence. I noticed a farmer, clad in carpet-slippers and corduroys, galloping along Aidensfield village street at six o'clock one morning. I was forlornly standing outside the telephone kiosk making a point, having been on an abortive motorcycle patrol since 4.30 am, and wishing something would happen. This could be it! Trouble of some kind!

I watched his approach. He wove from side to side with his head down, his flat cap perched on the front of his head and his feet twinkling across the road surface as he panted towards me. Knowing I could help, whatever it was, I stepped forward and said, "Hello, Mr Stanhope, nice morning."

He slowed momentarily in his tracks, looked at me and said, "Aye," then darted into the kiosk.

Feeling snubbed, I stood at a discreet distance as he began his urgent telephoning. Several of the glass windows of the kiosk were broken and I could not help overhearing his words. It didn't take long for me to appreciate he was having trouble with the telephone. I could hear him shouting uselessly into the mouthpiece and it was evident there was a total lack of response. After two minutes of futile efforts, he emerged and addressed me.

"Mr Rhea, can thoo work this contraption?"

"I can, Mr Stanhope. What's the matter?"

"Ah've a cow aboot ti cawf and Ah need a vetinary. Ah've nivver used yan o' these new-fangled telephoning contraptions. Ah'll etti git him there sharp, she's very nigh due."

"Well," I said. "It's quite simple. You call the operator, ask for the number you require and then she'll tell you how much money to put in. You can see the coin-box just there. When the money's in, she'll ring the number and when you are connected you'll be told to press button 'A'. That's on the side of the box. Then you can talk."

"Oh," he said, obviously failing to comprehend my advice. I knew I'd have to show him. I exhorted him to enter the cramped box and I followed, squeezing him inside as I stood at the entrance holding the door open with my foot. This was in the days long before decimalisation and long before STD became commonplace in telephone-boxes. Those kiosks were solid edifices with a large money-box inside and a little tray to help get your money back, if the call was not connected.

"Ah see's where Ah've been gahin wrang," he laughed. "Ah thowt there was a choice of prices. Ah thowt Ah'd 'ave t'cheapest on offer. Ah mean, a penny's nowt is it?"

I knew the coin-box had "penny", "sixpence" and "shilling" written on the top, with appropriate slots for each coin. I didn't know what he'd done so far, but he seemed to be coping. I dialled "O" to link him with the operator and left him to it. He had a pile of coppers on top of the coin-box and seemed content.

"Number please," I could hear the strident voice of the lady operator.

"Hello," he shouted. "Hello, Ah want oor vetinary."

"Which veterinary?" I heard her ask.

"That'un that cums tiv oor farm ivvery Thursday," he said blandly.

"Look, sir," the girl replied in a softer voice. "I need to know his number before I can put you through."

"Number?" gasped the farmer. "He hasn't gitten a number, has he? He's nut a convict or a policeman or owt like that. Our policeman's gitten a number on his shoulder, but oor vetinary hasn't . . ."

"No, sir, his telephone number . . ."

"Nay, lass, Ah knows nowt about that, that's your job. Look, just git hod on him and send him along. Ooor Primrose is gahin ti cawf and he's needed there right sharp. She's very restless, thoo knaws."

17

"Who is that calling, sir? I will try to find a veterinary surgeon for you . . ."

"Stanhope from Aidensfield."

"And where is the trouble, Mr Stanhope?"

"In my cow-shed. If he doesn't get there quick, I fear for t'awd lass."

"I appreciate that, but where is your cow-shed?"

"Next ti t'pig-sties. We've gitten fifteen pig-sties and yon cow-shed's right next door . . ."

"No, I mean your address! Where shall I send the vet if I find him?"

"Oh, just to our farm. Stanhope, tell him. Me and my family's been farming there for generations. Tell him Stanhope, he'll know where to come."

"But I don't know which is your vet, Mr Stanhope . . ."

"Oh, it's young Singleton from Ashfordly."

"Look, Mr Stanhope, you get along home and I'll ring Mr Singleton for you. It's a cow that's calving, and she's in your cow-shed. Now, what's your address?"

"High Brow Farm. He can't miss it, thoo knows and any rooad, he's been before."

"All right, Mr Stanhope. You get along and I'll ring him."

"Thanks, miss," he said.

He replaced the handset and emerged happily, collected his pile of unused pennies from the top of the coin-box and grinned at me.

"Well?" I asked.

"Grand," he grinned wickedly. "Grand. Yon telephone lass is telling Singleton to get himself there as sharp as he can."

"So things will be right, eh?"

"Aye," he said, "things'll be right. Nice awd cow is our Primrose. Thoo'll be coming along to have a look at her, eh? There'll be a cup of tea about seven, I reckon, after t'vet's done his stuff."

"Thanks," I said. "I'll look forward to that."

"Think nowt on it," he said. "Yon phone call cost me nowt, did it?" He smiled craftily. "I reckon you and me's earned our cup of tea this morning."

As he stomped away, I wondered what this early morning encounter had proved. I hadn't dealt with a major police crisis but, somewhere, crafty old Stanhope had taught me a lesson in Yorkshire thrift.

# CHAPTER TWO

Men are suspicious; prone to discontent.
ROBERT HERRICK, 1591—1674

Like any other organised body of people and equipment, the police service cannot afford to stand still. Progress must be allowed to intrude and interfere and, because many police officers are essentially conservative in their outlook and stubborn to boot, change comes by being forced upon them. Initially, many attempt to reject this but the mighty feet of officialdom stamp forward until, by dint of enforced usage and repeated orders from above, the necessary change is effected. By then, it is time for another.

Policemen everywhere do not agree that change or progress constitutes improvement. Progress implies a move forward, but that in itself is not necessarily an improvement. Within the service, changes are made frequently. Progress is moderately common and improvement a rarity.

It can be argued with some justification, therefore, that the concept of Unit Beat Policing and the accompanying Collator system was "progress", its arrival undoubtedly a useful change. For that reason it can be regarded as progress. Whether it was an improvement is for history and crime statistics to decide.

The system was designed for town and city policemen, but it was based upon the ideals of rural policing. The focal point of the system was a constable who lived on his patch. He was provided with a car in which to patrol and a back-up force to aid him in his duties. Basing this idea on the notion that rural bobbies know everyone and everything that happens on their patch, the pundits reckoned the same logic could apply to a city area if the area had its own constable. And so the Unit Beat system was born. To assist the constable living in pseudo-rural bliss among slag heaps and council houses, he was allocated a team of panda car drivers to patrol the area. They were to deal with matters of urgency and transport the resident bobby around and there was a plain-clothes man from the C.I.D. He sorted out the villains on the patch. Between them, these men policed their Unit and spent time getting to know everything and everyone. In theory, it was masterly.

The snag was that it didn't quite work like that. It is quite impossible to transplant rural systems into city environments. City people are a different breed and do not react or behave like countryfolk. And, furthermore, one car cannot do the work of five men. The result was that every police force developed its own interpretation of the Unit Beat system and few of them benefited from it.

One redeeming feature, however, was the Collator and his concomitant indexing system.

There was nothing original in having a comprehensive index and in fact most rural beat constables used their own excellent systems. The problem was that they filed most of the information in their heads. They knew who got up early, who came home late, which car belonged to whom and whose wife was seeing someone else's husband. They knew the villains and the goodies, the perverts and the businessmen. In short, they knew a lot. If a constable left the vicinity, he took all his information with him. That was the problem because the new man had to start all over again. If only all that information was recorded . . . With this idea of bliss in mind, Home Office experts created the Collator. This was merely a man with a filing system. He used reference cards, strip indexes and other office requisites to keep tabs on the villains and ne'er-do-wells. The basic idea was sound. It said that every policeman who patrolled a Unit Beat area would make a written note of what he saw. If, for example, he observed Burgling Bert from Bridlington walking along Albany Street at 6 o'clock one morning and carrying a walking-stick, he would note that fact in his police notebook. He would then enter the fact in the Collator's files, probably under the name of Burgling Bert. Gradually a file would grow and the Collator would have a complete record of Burgling Bert's movements should anyone wish to run a check on his activities at any time. The system was useful because it could identify a villain, but, if correctly compiled, it could also clear a suspect. It might prove the alibi of an innocent person.

Most rural beat constables ran a similar system long before the Home Office came up with its mind-boggling advance and I kept my own record of events on Aidensfield beat.

It was through my system that I became very suspicious of John Henry Tyler. It must be said at the outset that, in spite of this new and revolutionary aid to common sense, I would have become suspicious of the fellow. Recorded facts cannot lie; John Henry Tyler was up to something and my files proved it.

He was a retired hill farmer in his middle sixties who had come down from a remote part of the North Yorkshire moors to retire to Aidensfield. His wife was called Ruth and they kept a collie dog called Wade, named after the giant who lived near their farm years ago. John Henry was a stout man with a walk like a sailor and his shortness, when in motion, served only to give him the appearance of a trundling barrel. His face was round and jolly and it always wore two or three days' growth of whiskers. I wondered when he shaved, or how he shaved, in order to preserve this unkempt appearance. His clothing was rough and rural, practical perhaps but never smart. To complement his rustic countenance, he reeked of farmyards, middens and cow-sheds. He was a walking example of the scents of the English countryside.

Not once during my first few months at Aidensfield did I have any reason to suspect him of illegality. He taxed his car, licensed his dog, paid his rates and ensured that all his firearms documents were in order. He was the epitome of a worthy villager, true as they come and as straight as a newly fletched arrow.

Having been a hard-working and poorly paid hill farmer, he had been accustomed to rising very early and it was the continuance of this habit that drew my attention to him. Very early one morning, I was sitting astride my stationary motorcycle at the junction of Aidensfield village street and Elsinby Road. I could hear approaching footsteps and was tucked nicely beneath an overhanging conifer. I knew I was practically invisible so I remained very, very still in the shadows. I looked at my watch. It was 5.30 a.m.

Very soon, the oncoming footsteps materialised into the rounded shape of John Henry Tyler. His head was down against the fresh breeze of an early spring morning and he wore a muffler about his neck. On his feet were the traditional leather-topped clogs of the district and he wore the only coat I'd ever seen him use, a tatty, dull brown, sack-like affair with bulging pockets and a massive collar. His hands were deep in those commodious pockets, his chin was tucked into the ample collar and his feet were eating up the yards as he hurried about his early business.

He walked right past without seeing me. I observed that grizzled grey hair, the unshaven weather-beaten face and his rough country clothes as he hurried along the lane. John Henry hadn't changed in retirement. He still went about unshaven and smelling of cows and pigs. This morning was no exception. But he wasn't going to work, surely? Naturally, I was curious about his purpose, but didn't interrupt. Instead, I simply kept him under observation.

He turned right at the junction and hurried down the gentle gradient which led to Elsinby, two miles distant. I waited ten minutes before I left my vantage-point and took the motorcycle to the hilltop. From there, I could see John Henry's diminishing figure striding along the road. He was still heading towards Elsinby with his hands in his large pockets and his old head bowed against the chilly breeze. Where was he going? At this point, I never suspected his involvement in anything criminal. I took him to be an active countryman going for an early morning walk.

Over the following months, however, this event repeated itself many times. I noticed him on several occasions, always walking that stretch of road and always at this time of the morning. He was always dressed in his scruffy old clothes and clogs and never carried anything. Furthermore, I never saw him make a return journey. Mentally I had noted these sightings but now decided to record them in writing. Maybe they could be linked with some distant crimes? Had he a woman? Once or twice, I waited in Elsinby village but always missed him there. He seemed to vanish somewhere on the road between the two villages. One or two of my colleagues reported seeing him during their early morning patrols around my beat, but none saw him actually in Elsinby. This created even more interest.

The frequency of his trips bothered me too. My awkward shifts did not allow me to see him regularly, but by dint of asking my colleagues and checking from time to time myself the fact emerged that it was a monthly outing, usually on a Thursday.

I could not believe that John Henry was a criminal. He was not a criminal type, he was a stolid rural character, a bit sharp perhaps, but definitely not a villain. I had no reports of criminal activities on my beat with which he could be associated but I did check my Crime Bulletins just to be sure that there was nothing suspicious along my beat boundaries. I was very aware that a series of burglaries had been committed in widespread rural areas over a period of about two years and all had been perpetrated during the early hours of the morning. Collators over a large area had pooled their information, and as a result, an early morning worker from York was arrested. His practice was to hitch-hike out of town to his place of work, but this system sometimes provided him with spare time. He made profitable use of that time by breaking into houses. The mass of apparently unconnected intelligence gathered by the collators, eventually linked his movements with the burglaries and brought about his arrest. It was not impossible that old John Henry was perpetrating something highly illegal. Stranger things had happened, but I had to know. I had not to ask him directly, not yet. I must discover more about him and began discreet enquiries into his background. He lived in a rented house in Aidensfield with his wife and dog, and had never had children. His circumstances could be described as "poor". The farm he'd worked high on the North Yorkshire moors had also been rented, and throughout his life he had worked from morning until night, scraping the barest of livings from that tough moorland area. He'd kept a few sheep and half a dozen milking cows and he had grown root-crops in a small enclosure surrounded by a dry-stone wall. My sources told me his income had never exceeded £11 per week. John Henry was indeed a poor man, but proud. If he'd existed all his life in this manner, it was barely credible that he'd turn to crime in his retirement.

Nonetheless, the fact that he had retired meant he would have little to live on. So was the old devil going stealing at dawn? It seemed a feasible theory and one which would impress Sergeant Blaketon, so I decided to intensify my observations and enquiries.

I checked all the reported burglaries, housebreakings, shop-breakings, larcenies, poachings and other crimes in the district and compared their times with the known movements of John Henry. It is fair to say that none could be positively attributed to him, but in some cases they could have been. Rather sorrowfully, I began to grow worried about him. I knew that if I made a good arrest, especially one which cleared up a spate of serious crimes, I would be in Sergeant Blaketon's good books for a time. I found myself regarding John Henry's movements as a key to my future. Through him, I could make a name for myself.

I knew I had to be cunning. I had to catch him either in the act or with the stolen property. It was little use going about the place on the noisy Francis Barnett as that would alert him so I crept out of the house on several mornings and went about furtive foot patrols. I kept to the shadows, to the fields and woods as I attempted to keep an eye on this early morning clog walker.

Finally, there came a moment of triumph. I was concealed behind an old building alongside the Aidensfield-Elsinby road when I heard the familiar clip-clop of his clogs. It was a lovely summer morning with the birds singing and the scent of blossom in the air; it was most certainly not a time to be engaged in furtive criminal activities, but, sure enough, John Henry was heading my way.

I watched him from the security of the building. His head was down in that familiar style and his hands were tucked deep into those huge pockets as he stomped along the road. I waited until he was fifty yards ahead of me and began to shadow him. I used the heavily-leaved hedges and copses as my shelter as I moved stealthily along the fields. I readily kept pace with the active old man and he never once turned to look my way. I got the impression that he was deep in thought, his mind a long way from this peaceful stretch of England.

I shadowed him all the way to Elsinby where he arrived just before six o'clock. But instead of entering the village street he turned sharp left and for a moment I lost him. Blast! He'd tricked me! In order to catch him I had to scramble out of the fields and regain the road, and I did so with considerable effort and anxiety. Eventually, I landed muddy-footed on the highway, panting slightly and with my cap at an angle. I hurried after him into the village, but he'd vanished. He'd got away! The cunning old devil!

He could only have gone one way and that was along the lane to Ploatby, so that was the road I took. But even before I'd gone fifty yards a car emerged from one of the cottages along that road. It was a nice tan Rover 2000 driven by a smart gentleman and in the front passenger seat was none other than John Henry Tyler.

It was past before I could stop it and I was rewarded by a wave from both men as the car vanished through the village towards York. I knew the owner of that car — he was a Mr Eugene Peterson, a retired wealthy businessman from Croydon. It was a most unlikely partnership, so what was going on?

The mysterious pair vanished from my sight with no attempt to conceal their departure, so I now wondered if Peterson was a high-class villain, perhaps a con-man, using old Tyler as a stooge? It was not beyond the bounds of credibility.

Deflated, I was now faced with a long walk back home and my efforts had produced very little more information, except I now knew the identity of his partner in crime. Back in my office an hour later, I rang York's collator to see if there was any record of that car in their files, but there wasn't. It had never come to the notice of York Police in a suspicious manner, nor had its occupants. Either they were very clever criminals or they weren't criminals at all.

I was now faced with several probabilities and several different ways of tackling the problem. Certainly, something unusual was going on. There was no doubt about that and it was my duty as the local constable to unearth the truth. If I told Sergeant Bairstow, he'd laugh it off, and Sergeant Blaketon would wheel them both in for interview. Neither seemed the right approach. I had to find out for myself and then tell the sergeants. I could be bold and ask them outright to account for their movements, but, if they were engaged in crime, that would alert them to police interest and we'd never solve anything.

The only solution was to make discreet enquiries in Elsinby and the finest starting-place for such delicate questions was the Hopbind Inn. Later that morning, I made it my first calling-place and George produced a cup of warm coffee. It was just ten o'clock.

"Busy?" he asked, by way of opening the conversation along official lines.

"So, so." I shrugged my shoulders, hoping he'd accept that as an indication of the non-urgent nature of my presence.

"You're early — it's usually dinner-time when you get here." Dinner-time for Yorkshire folk is lunchtime for other people.

"Aye." I sipped the coffee as I perched on a stool in his bar. He wiped many glasses. "Tell me, George, do you know Eugene Peterson, the chap with the Rover?"

"Aye, I do," he said, looking earnestly at me.

"What sort of chap is he?" I continued. We were alone.

"All right," said George. "Honest, quite well-off, I'd say. Grown up family, retired businessman. Pleasant enough chap."

"Honest?"

"I'd say so. I've never heard anything against him."

I didn't respond but savoured his coffee so now he came at me with:

"Come along, Mr Rhea, what's on your mind? Is he up to something?"

"I don't know," I said wistfully. "I don't know, but I must find out."

"Why, what's he done?"

I knew I could trust George's discretion, so I unfolded my catalogue of early suspicions about John Henry Tyler and now Eugene Peterson. George listened carefully, wiping more glasses and sipping occasionally from his own coffee.

He smiled as I unfolded my yarn, his smile broadening as I enlarged my tale. I could see he was amused and knew, at that point, that my two suspects were not criminals.

"So, there it is, George. What's going on?"

"You've no idea, have you?" he grinned wickedly.

"No," I said, "I haven't."

"Well, every third Thursday in the month, John Henry walks down here and goes off in Peterson's Rover. They go to York Railway Station and catch an early train to London."

"Go on," I encouraged him.

"Well, you might believe this of Peterson, but not your John Henry. You see, they're both top chess-players; they play international chess at a club in London. Some are postal contests, some are live, and I believe some are played over the telephone. Peterson introduced John Henry to the London club, and they go there every month. John Henry's loved down there!"

"John Henry Tyler? You mean that smelly old farmer is a major chess-player?"

"One of the country's best; you'll occasionally see his name in the posh Sundays — last year, he beat a Russian grandmaster . . ."

"But why doesn't he get dressed up?"

"He never dresses up for anything and he doesn't want the village to know about it. You won't tell anyone, will you? The club has agreed not to publicise his real identity, so don't let John Henry know that you're onto him. He'll kill me for letting his secret out."

Back in the office, I wrote "checkmate" on my file about John Henry Tyler.

* * *

It was the ubiquitous Shakespeare who called the milkmaid "Queen of curds and cream", while Sir Thomas Overbury in 1614 wrote, "In milking a cow and straining the teats through her fingers, it seems that so sweet a milk press makes the milk the whiter or sweeter."

These lovely rural ladies were considered the height of perfection and in days of yore were worshipped as the purest of creatures. When farms were run as highly competitive commercial enterprises, even ladies of standing regarded the job of milkmaid as worthwhile. It was never looked upon as a menial task and advice given to dairy farmers was to have a good breed of cow, to possess proper buildings and implements and to have an attractive and skilful dairymaid. One farmer, writing in the last century said, "It is a truly feminine employment and to their hands it (the milking) should be left." It was widely accepted that cows "never let their milk down pleasantly" to someone they dreaded or disliked and it was felt that cows enjoyed being soothed by mild usage, especially when ticklish and young. It was known that contented cows provided good creamy milk, and it was the job of the milkmaid to win the best from her bovine charges.

Although my beat embraced many dairy-farms, there were not many milkmaids in or around Aidensfield. To be truthful, I did not personally know one, but it seemed that there was such a beauty on a remote farm. One day I would meet her, I felt sure. The farm in question, a large dairy-farm on the moors beyond Briggsby, occupied a considerable but isolated site well away from the main road to Harrowby. I had called on a couple of occasions in the past to check the stock registers but never during those brief visits had I espied this renowned beauty.

Then late one evening, I received a telephone call at home. It was from Joe Camplin, the farmer in question. He sounded agitated and asked if I was on duty.

I wasn't, but asked if I could help.

"Aye, it's about Diane Ferguson," he said hesitantly.

"Diane Ferguson?" I didn't recognise the name.

"Aye, my milkmaid, the Scots girl, you know."

"Oh." I had never seen the girl, but the point registered. "Something wrong, Mr Camplin?"

"Aye, she's been attacked."

"Attacked?" I shouted. "Where?"

"Down our lane. Not five minutes ago . . ."

"Is she badly hurt?" I asked, wondering whether a rogue cow had attacked her or whether it was something else.

"No, but she's shaken. It was a man, grabbed her, he did. She got away though."

"I'll be there right away," I promised.

Although it was my day off, I jumped into my private car and rushed five miles to the lonely farm. As I drove through the countryside, I looked for a solitary man walking the lanes at night, but found no one. I hoped I might come across the culprit but out here a person can lose himself very rapidly. Near this farm, there is nothing but wide open moorland, interspaced with a few spruces and silver birch. He could be anywhere out there. My headlights found only dry-stone walls, solitary trees and the occasional cottage. As I turned down the lane to Crag Foot Farm, I discovered the unmade road was muddy and full of holes. It threatened to shake my car to pieces as I bumped and bounced along its terrible surface. Fortunately, the farm's exterior light was burning and guided me onto the concrete yard near the back door. It was a relief to come to a halt.

I hurried inside, pausing to knock but once and shouted my arrival. I knew the way and rushed inside. In the comfortable kitchen I found Joe and Mary Camplin fussing over a tearful girl. This was Diane Ferguson.

"Ah," said Joe as I entered. "Thank God I found you in."

"How is she?" was my first question.

The girl smiled weakly through her tears and wiped her red eyes with a man's handkerchief, doubtless supplied by Joe. "I'm all right, thanks. Just shaken."

"Cup o' tea?" suggested Mary Camplin. "I've made one for Diane."

"Thanks," I accepted her offer and pulled out a chair to settle at the table. The tea was lovely.

"I heard her come crying into the yard," began Joe before I could ask what had happened. "It was dark, and she'd run all the way . . . he got her by the throat . . ."

"Let's start at the beginning, eh?" I suggested, turning my attention to Diane. She was a petite girl, about twenty years old, very pretty with mousy hair and a face bearing a suggestion of freckles. Her delightful grey eyes were sharp and alert, her smile tantalising, and all were complemented by her figure which was charming and full. She looked more like a farm secretary or a shorthand typist than a milkmaid, but her appearance and demeanour reminded me of the charm of her Shakespearian counterparts. If poets and writers said that milkmaids were charming, this one proved the truth of their words.

"Tell me, Diane. What happened?"

"Well, Mr Rhea." Her accent contained a beautiful Lowland lilt. "It was like this. I got off the bus at the lane end," and she indicated the direction with her hands. "I always get off there, you see . . ."

"It's her afternoon off," butted in Joe. "She goes to Harrowby for the afternoon and gets that bus back. It stops at the lane end, just up the road from here."

"I see," I smiled and bade her continue. "You got off the bus. What time?"

"Half past eight, Mr Rhea. It was right on time."

"Go on."

"Well, it was dark, you see, and I had a torch. I got off like I always do, and began to walk down the lane to the farm . . ."

"I've often said I should put a light at that lane end," commented Joe. "I'll do it now, by God I will."

I smiled at Diane. She understood and we tolerated his well-intentioned interruptions.

"Well," she continued. "I got as far as the haystack . . ."

"I always put a stack in that field," said Joe. "It's handy for my cows when they're up there . . ."

"Joe, shut up," ordered his wife. "Let Mr Rhea talk to Diane."

"Oh, sorry," he said, picking up his cup of tea.

"I'd just got past the stack when a man jumped out at me," the girl said slowly. "I didn't know what to do . . . I didn't run . . . I think I was too frightened . . . I just didn't know . . ."

"What did he do?" I put this important question gently but firmly. I had to know whether there'd been any attempt at rape or indecent assault. It mattered for my subsequent action.

"He tried to put a sack over my head," she said, wiping away a tear. "A dirty old sack . . ."

"A sack?"

"Yes, it sounds so silly, but he had a sack. It was a rough hessian one, all smelly and horrible, and he tried to put it over me . . . I began to run, but he grabbed me by the arm . . . he was very strong, so I shouted and screamed . . ."

"He didn't touch you?" I asked. "Indecently, I mean? Or say anything?"

She shook her head. "No, nothing like that, thank God. It was just that sack . . . I fought and fought, but he was very strong."

"And you screamed?" I sipped at the tea.

"Yes, but the farm's too far away for Mr and Mrs Camplin to hear me and the bus had gone by then. No one heard me. There was nobody."

"So what did you do?"

She hesitated. "I kicked him, right between the legs," and she laughed. "I knew it hurt — he called out in pain, and then I hit him with my torch." She showed me the cracked glass.

I smiled at her bravery. "Great! That'll teach him a lesson. Then what happened?"

"He ran away," she smiled at the memory, "and I came in here, crying. Mr Camplin went out . . ."

"I did that, with my shotgun. If I'd seen him in our lane he'd have got both barrels right up his backside, I can tell you."

"And you found no one?"

"Not a soul." He shook his head.

"And the sack?"

"Nay, lad, I didn't see that. I was too concerned about Diane."

"Did he say anything to you?" I asked her again.

"No, nothing. He just panted and grunted as he tried to put the sack over me. It's so silly . . . maybe he didn't mean any harm . . ."

"It was an assault if nothing else," I said. "Now, Diane, you had your torch. Was it on?"

She nodded.

"And could you see him? I need a description if you can give one."

She had no trouble providing me with a marvellously detailed description of her assailant. He was about 50 years old with thick grey hair, about average height, and he wore a dark donkey jacket with leather shoulder-patches. He had dark trousers, dark shoes, and a flat cap, checked style, with the press-stud undone above the peak. And he had a squeaky voice. She'd noted that as he'd cried out with pain. He was clean-shaven, she said, but whiskery, as if he'd not shaved for a day or two. He wore a white scarf and gloves with string backs, like racing drivers wore.

It was a first-class description and if this man lived in the district I would have little trouble tracing him. We'd trace him in no time.

"Have you any idea who it was?" I put to her. Quite often, unprovoked assaults of this kind were an outcome of some recent disagreement with a boyfriend or prospective suitor. Diane was a very pretty young woman, and must have had lots of suitors, so this could be some form of revenge.

"Yes, I think so," she said quietly.

"Aye," said Joe. "We think we know who it is. Nasty business, Mr Rhea. I don't want to be one to cause trouble, but it'll have to be stopped. Innocent girls can't be put at risk, you know . . ."

"So who is it?" I ventured.

"You know that Frenchman who lives up the hill, on the road to Harrowby?"

I shook my head.

"No, you wouldn't, he's like you, not been here all that long, but he took Blackamoor House as a studio. He's an artist, a clever chap, but a bit weird."

"Weird?" I asked.

34

"Well, not like us. Dresses queer, dyes his hair, smells of scent and stuff. It wouldn't surprise me if he had a bath every day neither."

"Artists often do dress individually," I said. "Has he been a nuisance before?"

"No," she said. "No, he never bothers me."

"So you're acquainted?"

"Aye," said Joe. "He comes here for his milk. Two pints a day — he collects them himself, in a little can like they do in France."

"What's his name?"

"Edouard Sannier," said Mary Camplin. "Monsieur Edouard Sannier. He's quite nice, I think. At least, I used to think he was."

"Now, Diane, listen carefully," I put to her. "Are you sure it was him? If I had to get you to swear on oath that it was Edouard Sannier would you say it was?"

"Yes," she said with a determined clenching of her teeth. "Yes, I would . . ."

"OK," I said. "I'll go and talk to him."

"What can you do with him?" Joe asked me.

"It's difficult to know what we can do," I said. "There was no indecency, and no attempt to rape Diane. He didn't say he was going to rape you, did he? There's no cuts, bruises?"

She shook her head.

"We're left with common assault, in which case you could take your own action against him. Common assault is not a matter for the police," I told them. "You go and see a solicitor and he'll fix it to go to court. If we consider he is a public nuisance," I added as an alternative, "we might get him bound over to be of good behaviour."

"I thought they'd send him to prison for what he did!" gasped Mary.

"For rape or attempted rape, yes, but for something like this, no. There's very little in law that can be done. Mind," I continued, "if he admitted he was going to rape Diane, or touch her indecently, we could consider a more serious charge. But first let me talk to him. I'll let you know how I get along. If I have to take him to the police station, it'll be morning before I see you."

"Aye, all right. I reckon Diane needs an early night," considered Joe, "with a drink of hot milk and whisky. She'll sleep on that."

"Couldn't be better. Now, Diane, is there anything else I should know? Did he say anything or do anything else? Have you angered him at all? Led him on, teased him?"

"No, honest, I've never given him any encouragement. Never . . ."

"These Frenchmen are very romantic, you know." I tried to make the incident sound light to reduce its seriousness, but I failed. For these people, it was a most serious event.

"It's not romance when they put bloody sacks over lasses' heads!" growled Joe.

I left them and drove the few hundred yards to the lonely cottage on the hilltop. A light was burning, which pleased me. I had never been into this house although I had passed it several times. Feeling apprehensive about the interview, I parked my car on the main road, walked to the studded front door and knocked. A pretty middle-aged lady answered, smiling up at me. She was very petite and charming.

"Yes?" she said pleasantly.

"Oh, I am P.C. Rhea," I introduced myself. "Is Monsieur Sannier in, please?"

"Yes, do come in." There was no trace of a French accent. In fact, she had a very English voice and I estimated she would be in her late sixties.

She led me into the lounge where I saw a grey-haired man sitting on the settee, sipping coffee. He rose as I entered.

"I am P.C. Rhea, the village policeman at Aidensfield," I announced. "I wonder if I could have a word with you, sir." I probably sounded very formal.

"But of course," he smiled and indicated an easy-chair. "It is always nice to meet the local policeman, eh, Alice?"

"Yes, dear," smiled his wife. "Would you like a coffee, Mr Rhea?"

"Er, no thanks," I refused as I settled in the chair. "I've just had one actually. Now, it's a very difficult enquiry for me . . ."

"We are very civilised," he said graciously. "It is trouble?"

His English was impeccable too, but he did have a high-pitched voice.

"Mr Sannier," I anglicised his title. "Where were you tonight, about eight-thirty?"

"Tonight? Why here, of course. With my wife."

"You didn't go out?"

"No, he did not," she said grimly. I paused deliberately as I looked around the small room. A piano stood against one wall and on top was a flat cap with the press-stud undone, a pair of gloves with string backs and a long white scarf. Hanging on a hook behind the door was a dark donkey jacket with black leather shoulder-patches and he had a thick mop of grey hair. Diane's description was perfect. It fitted him absolutely, although I'd have placed his age nearer sixty than fifty.

But was it too perfect? Everything matched and she had said he called regularly at the farm for his milk.

"Mrs Sannier, could you swear your husband did not leave the room this evening?"

She regarded me seriously. "We both went out, in our car, down to Ashfordly and returned in time for tea, just before five o'clock. Edouard went out to fill the coal-scuttle at six o'clock, and we've not been out since, neither of us. I will swear to that." She spoke in a fiercely protective manner.

"I believe you," I said, for it was true. I did believe them. This man was no putter of sacks over the heads of young nubile girls.

"What is it?" he asked, with a genuine interest. "Have I done wrong?"

I was in two minds whether to tell him. I didn't want to give the impression that I believed he'd do such a thing and yet I did owe the couple some explanation. As I dithered for a moment, Mrs Sannier poured a coffee and said, "I think this would help." She passed it to me and I relaxed in the chair.

I told them the full story as Diane had related it, and included the description she'd given. When I had finished, he laughed, "She described me, eh? You had to come."

"I had to come," I said. "But it seems a strange tale for a girl like Diane to concoct, Mr Sannier. I'm sure she was attacked."

"Maybe she is telling the truth," said his wife. "When I was washing the tea things, I saw a young man walking down the road towards the dairy-farm. He wore a dark donkey jacket, just like Edouard's, and a flat cap, and a long light-coloured scarf with string-back gloves. I remembered thinking how like Edouard he looked."

"What time was that?" I felt excited.

"Six o'clock," she said. "Perhaps a minute or two either way, but near enough to six."

That was two and a half hours *before* the attack. "Tell me more," I said.

"Well, he comes down the road every Wednesday night. He walks into Ashfordly to the pub. I think he works on the Forestry Commission land near Sutton Bank Top."

"Do you know his name?" I asked.

"Sorry," she said. "I don't."

"Well, I'll have to make some more enquiries," I said. "Look, I'm very sorry to have troubled you like this — I feel very guilty about ruining your evening."

"Think nothing of it, young man," said Monsieur Sannier. "In some countries, I would have been dragged off and clapped in jail for less. I hope you find the man."

There are times one has to trust a man almost on sight and I trusted this one. I was convinced he had nothing to do with the attack on Diane.

To cut a long story short, I went straight to the private address of the Forestry Commission boss for the district and explained my problem. He told me he knew the lad, a twenty-two-year-old who lived with his parents in a woodland cottage a mile from the top of Sutton Bank. The parents kept a smallholding with hens and pigs but the lad was very shy with girls. He was totally unable to communicate with them, so he was a likely candidate. The description supplied by Mrs Sannier fitted him.

Knowing I would have difficulty locating him tonight, I went to the cottage in the woods first thing next morning. I found Jeremy Morley at home. His dad was labouring on a farm nearby and mother was out. He allowed me in; it was a hovel and filthy with it, but for this unfortunate lad it was home. And there, on a hook behind the door was a dark donkey jacket, a flat cap with the peak button undone, a dull white scarf and, on the table, a pair of driving-gloves with string backs.

Almost before I began my questioning, the lad readily admitted trying to capture the girl. He knew it was best to put sacks over the heads of captured birds to calm them; he'd seen his dad do it many times with hens. And he'd seen the television, where men carried off the girl of their choice. He thought he'd do the same. He'd waited two hours behind that haystack, knowing Diane got off the Harrowby bus each Wednesday, and said he liked the look of her. He'd never spoken to her — he didn't dare, and he'd dressed up like Monsieur Sannier because he liked the Frenchman's style and confidence. That man knew how to treat girls, he felt, so he copied his idol for style and his father for action. I don't think he realised it was wrong.

After speaking to Sergeant Bairstow about it, we took the lad to court and he was bound over to be of good behaviour. The court persuaded him to seek treatment for his loneliness and appalling shyness in the face of girls. Diane forgave him too, which helped, and she went up to the Sanniers' cottage to apologise for implicating the unfortunate man.

Although I was pleased we found the culprit, I was even more pleased that I hadn't prosecuted the wrong man. It would have been so easy to ruin the Sanniers' life but I did wonder about the calming influence of hessian sacks upon one's head!

## CHAPTER THREE

"Is there anything to which you wish to draw my attention?"
"To the curious incident of the dog in the night-time."
"The dog did nothing in the night-time."
"That was the curious incident," remarked Sherlock Holmes.
ARTHUR CONAN DOYLE, 1859—1930

When I walked in the garden of my hilltop police house, I could look upon the expanse of the valley between and watch the passing show. One outcome of my elevated rural studies was an appreciation of the variety of farm animals that lived and worked on my patch.

There were horses of every kind. They ranged from the massive Shires and Clydesdales being bred for show purposes, to the diminutive Shetland ponies loved by little girls having riding-lessons. The cows included everything from Red Polls to Friesians with bulls to keep them content, and there were pigs and sheep, dogs and cats, hens and guinea-fowl. Some farmers even bred rabbits, hamsters, goats and donkeys. One striking fact was that all these beasts lived happily side by side and seemed in joyful communion with the wild creatures that occupied the same parcel of countryside.

It would be nice if all races of men could live in such harmony, but we must recognise that animals are not emotional creatures. They eat and sleep, they make love and they make war, but they do not worry about their image, neither do they stalk their portion of England believing that brown cows are superior to whites, that stallions should wash up, or that moles should fight for equal rights with squirrels. In spite of their minor quarrels, they are a happy bunch, and it is fair to say that no animal, of its own volition, caused me professional anxiety. Interest, yes; curiosity, certainly, but apprehension — no!

Some of their owners did and some of the animals did when affected by the behaviour of their humans. One professional problem surrounded a beautiful black Labrador called Nero. Really, it wasn't his fault at all, but it was alleged that he became savagely involved with a flock of sheep owned by a fiery farmer called Fairclough. This was Donald Fairclough of The Grange, Thackerston.

During the early months of my constableship at Aidensfield, I had experienced very little contact with Donald Fairclough because Mr Fairclough had taken it upon himself to be a gentleman farmer. He wore hacking-jackets, plus-fours and brogues. Locally, the term "gentleman farmer" suggests a rich man who owns a farm but who pays someone else to do the work and talk to policemen. Mr Fairclough's wealth allowed him to spend a lot of time overseas or riding about the countryside in his Daimler with two golden retrievers and a shotgun at his side. Had anyone witnessed his demeanour, dress and dogs, he would immediately classify him as a gentleman farmer. He was that sort of person, although I believe he grew up in Middlesbrough.

Being Mr Fairclough of Thackerston Grange made him feel rather important and he perpetuated his personal image by talking loudly, telephoning incessantly and writing incomprehensible letters to newspapers and parish councils. His turnover of domestic and farm staff was rapid, and it was rumoured that sometimes he had to return to his lovely farm personally to feed the pigs or muck out the cows when a walk-out occurred. But such events were rare — he had enough money to find someone to do the job in return for a quick pound or two in cash. Donald Fairclough always got by.

It was during my first spring at Aidensfield that I experienced the wrath of his tongue. My telephone rang in the middle of a Wednesday afternoon when, I happened to be at home between shifts. Mary answered it and informed me it was a Mr Fairclough who sounded important and upset.

"Hello!" boomed the voice. "Is that the policeman?"

"P.C. Rhea," I identified myself.

"Sheep-worrying," shouted Fairclough. "Some bloody dog's attacked my flock of black-faces."

"When?" I asked.

"Recently, very recently," returned the voice. "My man's just come down from my ten-acre. There's five sheep mauled and one dead. Savaged by a bloody dog. Get yourself down here straight away."

I was tempted to reply "Yes, sir" but resisted. Fairclough wasn't going to have me running around in circles.

Even so, sheep-worrying is one of the most terrible of rural happenings and I felt sorry for him. Anyone who fails to appreciate the horror of this all-too-common tragedy should take a look at a savaged sheep. They should think about a living animal with its intestines torn from its throbbing body by bloodthirsty domestic dogs whose normal senses have evaporated in a mist of raw meat smells. They should witness the terrified huddle of mangled animals who survive the onslaught, they should see the aborted lambs, dead even before they see separate life, and they should witness the tears in the eyes of tough, unemotive farmers who weep at the appalling sight. The agony is everyone's.

Sheep-worrying is much more than dogs running after stupid woollybacks. It is unbridled savagery at its worst; it is flocks of sheep which can be literally terrified into death; it is individual animals being eaten alive and it is humans claiming, "My dog could never do that." But it can, and so often does.

Fortunately, most rural folk understand the horrible nature of sheep-worrying and seek effectively to control their dogs. Some do not care, however, and, in addition, many newcomers to the countryside do not comprehend the dangers caused by roaming Fidos and wandering Fluffs. In recent years, it has been observed that sheep who live near towns and city suburbs are being savaged by urban dogs whose owners turn them loose for walkies. Nationwide, it is a massive problem; for anyone living near sheep, it is a harrowing and ghastly crime.

I knew the problems only too well, having been nurtured in a moorland sheep-farming district, and I knew just how difficult it can be to locate the guilty dogs. If they are not found, they kill again and again. It is sometimes possible to analyse the stomach contents of suspect dogs or examine the hair about their muzzles in an effort to prove they had eaten living tissue from sheep. Positive proof is required but so often the guilty dogs escape and are never found, even though they return to savage the flocks time and time again.

It is a harrowing period for the farmer when a killer dog is at large and for the rural policeman it can prove a severe test of his skills in tracing suspects, even those of the four-legged variety. It is a battle which must be won. It was with some trepidation, therefore, that I motored along the lane to Thackerston Grange.

Fairclough must have heard the distinctive note of my motorcycle because he was waiting in his farmyard. I parked the machine against a saddle, removed my crash-helmet and left it on the pillion.

"Fairclough." He held out his hand and we shook on this, our first official encounter. I had seen him striding about Ashfordly from time to time and we'd nodded a kind of greeting on occasions. But this was business.

He indicated a tractor and said, "Jump on."

Soon he was guiding the noisy machine down the lanes between his expansive fields with me perched on the back, hanging on for grim death to a mudguard.

"Glad I caught you in," he shouted above the noise.

"You caught me between shifts," I shouted back. "Normally, I'd have been out and you'd have missed me."

"You fellows are fully modernised these days, what with radios and motorcycles. I'd have found you. But I miss the copper who walked. Sad days when those chaps disappeared. Ah, here we are."

I hadn't time to point out it would have taken half an hour for me to walk to his farm, because we had arrived at a gently sloping field on the western limits of his farm. He shouted at me, "Open the gate, will you?"

I dropped from the tractor, opened the wooden gate and admitted the noisy machine. He brought it to a halt just inside and stopped the engine before climbing down.

"Over there." He pointed to a corner of the field where the hawthorn hedge was sufficiently robust to frustrate penetration by the most determined fleeing ewe. As we walked towards the corner, I could see the mass of bloodstained wool, some of it writhing painfully in a weird silence.

"There," and his voice softened. The most hard-headed farmer would show genuine sorrow at such a sight, and we both knew there was no way to save the lives of these mutilated animals.

"The vet's coming to put 'em to sleep," he said, "but I know you need to record what happened, for court."

"Of course. When did this happen?"

"Today, sometime between eleven this morning and two this afternoon."

Out came my notebook and I noted that there was one dead ewe, with its belly eaten away and its flesh torn into shreds. It had died an agonising death and it was possible to see the teeth-marks on the remaining skin. Protruding from its body was the half-eaten carcase of an unborn lamb.

The other five victims were lying in a huddle where they had fled, all severely mutilated about the belly region, with their innards protruding and their unborn lambs killed. All were in a state of severe shock and terror. It was impossible at this stage to say how many more of the remainder, now huddled beneath a clump of trees in a far corner, would suffer abortions as a result of being stampeded by the killer dog or dogs.

I made note of the injuries to these ewes and, with Fairclough's permission, cut a small strand of wool from each savaged sheep. I placed these into six plastic packets, all labelled.

"What's that for?" he asked with genuine interest, his voice subdued.

"If we find the dog and the owner denies it was loose at the material time, we might find traces of wool about its mouth or teeth. This can be matched with the wool I've taken from these animals."

"Thanks," he said.

"Well," I said. "These poor creatures will have to be put out of their misery."

"They'll not be feeling much pain now — the shock's numbed them. You'll see how they didn't try to flee from you. Poor devils — they're finished."

"But the vet will see to them?"

"He will, and soon."

We turned and walked away from the carnage. The brisk spring breeze wafted a nauseating smell towards me, the stench of death mingled with the unmistakable aura of sheep. It was gone in a second, but ever since that day I have linked the scent of raw mutton with sheep-worrying of the most horrifying kind.

"Well," I said as I regained the platform of the tractor. "All I need is a dog."

"It's a black Labrador," he said firmly. "Come into the house and we'll talk."

His house was a picture. It was beautifully furnished with exquisite antiques and expensive carpets, all combining to produce an impression of opulence and style. For all his reputed faults, the fellow had taste. He led me into the kitchen and we sat at the long scrubbed wooden table. A girl appeared without being called.

"Coffee, or something stronger?" he asked as she hovered.

"I wouldn't say no to a good stiff whisky," I admitted, for the sight and smell of those suffering ewes had made me queasy.

"And me." He nodded at the girl and she obeyed his wish. Soon we were enjoying large whiskies in tumblers of cut glass.

"You mentioned a Labrador," I ventured.

"Yes," he sipped appreciatively, "a black one. It's the first time I've had sheep killed or mauled, but not the first time they've been chased. Around Christmas, a neighbour reported that a black Labrador had been chasing my sheep around the field, but it got away. Since then, several farmers have seen the dog wandering about their land, sometimes alone and sometimes with a young lad."

"You know the lad?"

"I do," he said. "Mind you, Mr Rhea, I'm not saying it has killed my sheep. All I'm saying is that I *suspect* it has. I now pass those suspicions to you."

"Who is the boy?"

"You know Sidney Chapman?"

"Chapman?" I puzzled over the name. "Sorry, no."

"He doesn't get about, he's confined to a wheelchair. He lives in Valley View, the cottage with honeysuckle over the front door, just down the road from here."

"Right on the roadside?"

"That's the one."

"I know it." I knew the house, but not the man. "And that's the home of the dog?"

"Yes, his son, Jeremy, often takes it out. He's at school, a lad in his teens. Fifteen, I'd say."

"And the dog often goes out alone, eh?" I put to him.

"Aye, it does. Mrs Chapman works part-time in Malton, mornings, that is, and I do know the dog gets away from poor Sidney. I appreciate his difficulty but I must consider my stock."

"You don't commit yourself, yet you seem positive it is that dog." I sipped from the glass.

"It's the only black Labrador in this village," he said firmly, letting me draw my own conclusion.

"I'll have words with him," I promised. "You'll be prepared to let us prosecute if necessary?"

"I'd be happy to see the dog destroyed first," he said firmly. "If he does that, I'll not worry about him going to court. I just want the dog stopped."

"Fair enough."

A prosecution under the Dogs (Protection of Livestock) Act of 1953 could not proceed without the written consent of either the Chief Constable, the owner of the livestock worried or the occupier of the land where it happened. Accordingly, I obtained a written statement from Mr Fairclough which I wrote in my notebook, and incorporated his willingness to authorise proceedings, if the dog was not destroyed.

Having attended to both that matter and the massive tumbler of whisky, I adjourned to the village and walked to Valley View. It was an old cottage with Yorkshire sliding windows and a rough rustic porch overgrown with honeysuckle. There was a green front door and green woodwork, but the door was standing slightly ajar. I knocked.

"Come in," called a voice from the depths. "First on the right."

"It's the policeman," I announced as I pushed open the door.

"It's about time you called to see me," he said even before I entered the room. "Your predecessor always popped in when he was passing. Made himself a coffee and one for me too. Regular caller, he was."

I pushed open the door of the living-room and found Mr Chapman before the cosy fire. A black Labrador lay curled at his feet, wide-awake, and its dark eyes watched me as I entered the room. It flapped its tail on the fireside rug as I walked in, then closed its eyes.

"He likes you," said the man. "Sit down, Officer."

He was reading a heavy volume on the History of World War I and placed it on his occasional table to greet me.

"Sidney Chapman," he said. "Forgive me not getting up. I leave the door ajar so I can shout at visitors."

"P.C. Rhea," I introduced myself and shook his hand. "I'm fairly new here."

"I knew we'd got a fresh bobby and was hoping you'd pop in. I like company, you see, being stuck here all day. I lost the use of these legs eight or nine years ago. Car accident — I'm lucky to be alive, they tell me. Look, if you want a coffee, the kettle's in the kitchen . . ."

He was a neat man in his middle fifties, I reckoned, with a head of sleek hair which was neatly trimmed. His face was narrow and sharp, with prominent cheek-bones and just a hint of pallor. He wore spectacles and seemed an intelligent man. I wondered how he'd earned his living before the accident. He was cheerful and affable and I liked him immediately.

"No thanks," I said, "but I'll get you one . . ."

"No, I've just had the electricity meter reader in, he had a coffee with me. Thanks — but next time . . ."

"Mr Chapman." Sorrowfully, I had to notify him of the unpleasant purpose of my visit. "I'm afraid I'm not here on a social visit. It's business."

"Oh dear, something wrong?" he looked at me with concern.

"I'm afraid so. I'm sorry we have to meet like this, but there's been a nasty case of sheep-worrying at Grange Farm, Mr Fairclough's place. He tells me a black Labrador has been wandering around his fields."

"But Nero wouldn't harm a fly!"

At the sound of his name, the dog's head rose and his ears became alert as his eyes scrutinised the man for signs of further activity. His tail thumped the rug as he waited for developments.

"Has he been out this morning or this afternoon?"

"No, Mr Rhea, he hasn't. I can swear to that."

"Your front door was open — could he have gone out without you knowing? Maybe sneaked out for ten minutes and back again before you realised it?"

He thought carefully, then shook his head.

"No, I could swear to it. I've been here all morning, and he's been with me. He never leaves me, Mr Rhea, unless our Ian takes him out for a run. He's my sole companion during the day . . . he's not a killer."

"Do you mind if I examine him?" I hated to imply that I didn't accept his word.

"No, of course not."

I approached the waiting dog and noticed his brown eyes upon me, but a word from Mr Chapman kept the animal on the floor. As I touched the broad top of his head, he rolled over onto his back, with his legs in the air and I obliged by tickling his stomach. He lay there, tongue lolling out and those dark, trusting eyes upon me as I quickly surveyed his underparts and legs. They were clean — there was no sign of mud or blood. I was pleased.

"Can I open his mouth?"

"He won't bite," said the owner with confidence.

I gripped the dog by his jaws and opened his mouth, pressing the flaps of skin away from his sharp white teeth and clamping my hand over his tongue. There was no blood and no wool adhering to his mouth area. The dog was as clean as a whistle. This was no killer.

"Well?" he asked.

"Clean," I said.

"Does that mean he's innocent?" he asked.

"It means I'm sure he is, Mr Chapman. I understand that a black Labrador has been roaming those fields, unaccompanied, and yours is the only one in Thackerston."

"Yes, he is. But he's not been out this morning. I'd swear to that in a court of law."

"Thanks. I'm obliged." I made as if to leave his home.

"Mr Rhea, I'm not one to hold this against you — you are doing your job, and I respect the law and all it stands for. You'll call again?"

"I will, Mr Chapman, and under better circumstances next time."

When I informed Fairclough of my actions and decision, he almost burst a blood-vessel.

"P.C. Rhea! You are failing in your duty if you believe that rubbish! Of course he'd say the dog hadn't been out! He would, wouldn't he? It would go home covered in blood and dirt, so he'd clean it up! Of course he would, anybody would, if only to check the dog for injuries . . . it's a natural action . . ."

"I'm sure it was never out of that house during the times your sheep were attacked," I stood my ground. "A cripple couldn't wash a dog clean, not a dog that size and not as clean as that one. I even had its mouth open — it was clean too. No wool about the teeth, nothing. That dog didn't worry your sheep, Mr Fairclough."

"So what happens now? What does the law propose to do about my sheep?"

"I'll report this to my superiors," I said, "and our men will keep observations. If you see any dogs on your land, perhaps you'd let me know."

"I'll shoot the bastards first," he said. "I can, can't I?"

"You can shoot a dog actually in the act of worrying sheep, or one which you know has been worrying them and is about to renew its attack. You can't shoot one which is running away afterwards."

"Why not, for God's sake?"

"It might not be the culprit, not if it's only seen running away. It could be another innocent dog."

"Aye, well, we all know the way to get round that, Mr Rhea. Now look, if any of my sheep are damaged again, I'll be in touch with your Chief Constable and I'll tell him of this conversation. I know that dog killed my sheep. It's your job to prove it."

He was building up for a shouting match, so I left him. There was little point in continuing the argument. I could understand his view, but I was convinced Mr Chapman was telling the truth. I could not ignore the fact, however, that Nero might have sneaked out through that open door. Chapman could have cleaned up the animal too. It was quite possible, but I couldn't work on surmise. I needed absolute proof.

For a week there was peace, and then, one Sunday morning, my telephone rang. It was Fairclough again and he was extremely agitated.

"Mr Rhea? That dog's been back. One sheep attacked and torn this time. The flock terrified out of their wits . . . get yourself right down to Chapman's and see that dog of his. It was seen again."

"What time did this happen?" I asked.

"Between ten o'clock and half-eleven."

"I'm on my way," I told him. It was quarter to twelve.

Fairclough was parading up and down his farmyard as I entered, and his face was a picture of anger and frustration. As I parked the motorcycle, he marched across with eyes blazing and in a foul mood.

"It's that bloody dog again, Mr Rhea, one of my men saw it." He pointed to a clump of distant sycamores. "It went over there — he gave chase but lost it. A black Labrador — *that* black Labrador, the one you cleared last time. It's it, right enough."

"I'll see Mr Chapman straight away," was all I could promise.

I left my motorcycle in his farmyard as I intended returning, and found the cottage door open as before. I knocked, shouted and was bade enter.

"Mr Chapman? It's P.C. Rhea."

"Come in, Mr Rhea."

As before, I found him in the cosy living-room with a warm fire blazing cheerily in the grate. And, as before, the big black Labrador lay at his feet, with its head on the hearth. It pricked its ears and thumped its tail on the rug, apparently its regular welcome to its master's callers.

"It's about the same subject as before," I told him and he pointed to a chair.

"When?" was all he asked.

"This morning, between ten o'clock and half past eleven."

"He's not been out Mr Rhea, I swear it. He's been here all the time."

"The door was ajar," I said. "He could have sneaked out — it would take only ten minutes to worry a sheep — less in fact. He lives very close to the farm."

"Look at him," and the unhappy man pointed to his dog. I crouched on my haunches to examine the animal and at my touch it rolled over and asked for its stomach to be rubbed. I obliged and at the same time examined its body for signs of blood and dirt. There was none. His fur was dry too, indicating it hadn't been recently washed.

"Are you alone?"

"Sally's in the kitchen, doing lunch," he said. "She and Ian went out to church this morning. I was alone from quarter past ten until half past eleven, and Nero never left this room. I'd swear to this in court if necessary. You must believe me."

"You were here *every* minute?" I put to him, quietly.

He paused and looked steadily at me. "No, to be honest, I wasn't. I went to the toilet about eleven o'clock."

"Upstairs?"

"No, out at the back. I can get there and back with my chair."

"And, without wishing to be crude, how long did that take?"

"Five or ten minutes," and I could see the sorrow growing in his eyes. Like me, he realised that Nero had had enough time to gallop out, worry a sheep and return to the house. It was highly unlikely, but it was possible. Practical policemen must always consider the possible. I knew, and Sidney Chapman knew, that Nero could be the culprit in

52

spite of his cleanliness. Perhaps he'd licked himself clean, or maybe never got dirty.

I looked again at the magnificent dog. There was not a mark upon him to suggest he'd been chasing sheep within the past hour or so. In spite of Fairclough, I was convinced this was not the guilty dog.

"Is it nasty, this sheep-worrying?" Sidney Chapman asked me.

"It's one of the most appalling things that can happen to an animal," I said and, with no further ado, I provided a graphic description of the sights I'd witnessed. I stressed the emotional anguish and financial problems it presented to a farmer, and the continuing threat if the guilty dogs were not halted.

"But Nero couldn't do that . . ." he said. "He couldn't. He's gentle and tame, a family pet. He's my companion, my only real pal, Mr Rhea. When everyone's out and I'm left alone, he's all I've got. I know he hasn't done this horrible thing. I know."

"I believe you," I said. "There's nothing on Nero to make me even suspect him. But a black Labrador's been seen near the attacked sheep, and he's the only one around here. He's the prime suspect."

"Mr Fairclough wouldn't make this up, would he? About it being a black Labrador, I mean."

"No, he'll be as anxious as anyone else to find the right culprit. If he blames the wrong one, the right one will return and continue its work, won't it. He'll not blame the wrong dog, Mr Chapman, that would be foolhardy."

"I'd like him to call and talk to me," said Mr Chapman, "perhaps you'd ask him to pop in?"

"I will," I promised.

I honestly felt this would be a good idea and within minutes I was back at the Grange talking to Mr Fairclough. I told him of my visit and of my opinions, which he ignored, and I then invited him to visit Sidney Chapman. If he went now, I suggested, he'd see the dog for himself.

He agreed. He stomped away without a word and I decided not to intervene at this stage. If there was to be a prosecution, I would play my part, but I could never believe this dog was the worrier.

I do not know what transpired between them, but two days later I received a telephone call from Mrs Chapman. She rang from a kiosk and asked me to pop in to see Sidney when I was passing. I made a point of calling that same day.

In the same room beside the same glowing fire, I found him alone. He was clearly distressed and in a very emotional state.

"Mr Rhea," he said. "I couldn't bear the thought that my Nero might be killing sheep and lambs. I know he was not the guilty dog, I know it, but he could have been, eh? He could have sneaked out when my back was turned, or done it when he was out with Ian . . ."

"I don't think it was him . . ." I began.

"I've stopped it all," he said, sniffing back unshed tears. "The vet came this morning."

"The vet?" I cried.

"He took him away, Mr Rhea. It will be painless, he said," and Sidney Chapman burst into a flood of tears. I didn't know what to do, and took the line of least resistance. I left him to his misery.

I told Mary about it and we both felt deep sorrow for the poor man. In my heart of hearts, I could never believe Nero was the culprit, but Sidney Chapman had taken a wise course. He'd had the dog destroyed, and so removed the cause of any future aggravation.

Four days later, Fairclough hammered angrily on my front door. I was in the middle of lunch and found him spluttering furiously on the doorstep.

"That bloody dog again!" he said. "Less than five minutes ago . . ."

"Which dog?" I asked him.

"That bloody black Labrador of Chapman's! Caught in the act! Two sheep this time, one dead. But I got the bastard, Mr Rhea. Both barrels. It's in the Land Rover."

And he stalked away to his Land Rover which was parked in my drive. I followed and, sure enough, there was a dead dog, a large handsome black Labrador. It had been killed by two blasts from a 12-bore gun and was a bloody mess around the head and neck.

"You've solved your problem, then?" I smiled at him.

"I have, and I want that man prosecuting. He ignored me."

"Which man?" I asked.

"Chapman — it's his bloody animal."

"It isn't," I said softly. "He had his dog put to sleep four days ago, Mr Fairclough. His only pal, his only pride and joy. But because you said it was his dog he had it put down by the vet. This isn't his dog."

Deep among the hairy mess, I found a collar and there, hidden beneath a thick coat of fur, was the owner's name and address. It was a newcomer to Elsinby, two miles away across the fields, a retired lady from Leeds.

"I'll prosecute her for allowing her dog to worry your sheep," I said.

"No." He shook his head and I could see he was shaken. "No, there's been enough damage. It's over — I'll seek compensation from the dog's owner, that'll do me. I'll go and see her now."

And he turned and drove away, a sad and thoughtful man.

A week later, he presented a new black Labrador pup to Sidney Chapman. When I called to see him a few weeks later, it had its head on the hearth and its tail thumped the rug, but only for a second.

It jumped up and fussed over me with all the vigour of youth. "He's called Caesar," Sidney told me as I went to make the coffee.

* * *

Although my professional duties involved all manner of farm animals, I did involve myself with canine matters more than

55

any other. It is true that dogs are an essential and integral part of village life, but the same could be said of cows, horses, pigs and sheep. I had to inspect small groups of these animals from time to time, either to count heads for record purposes or to see if I thought they had some disease that necessitated a veterinary surgeon's attention. I found it strange that a policeman's opinion was sought on such matters but invariably the problem was solved by ringing a vet.

It was one such problem that intrigued me at Cold Hill Farm, and it involved another dog. This was a cur, a common breed in these parts. They are used to guide sheep and are the hill farmer's constant companion. They are black and white dogs, tough and intelligent little animals with a natural instinct for herding sheep.

The resident cur at Cold Hill Farm was an elderly dog called Shep and he belonged to Mr and Mrs Ambrose Lowe. He had endured a long and hard life on this remotest of farms, spending his years herding moor sheep into their pens and rounding them up for their quarterly count. Year in, year out, poor old Shep had done those tasks and many more. Now he was twelve years old and I think he'd made his own decision to retire.

The snag was that Ambrose wouldn't let him retire. There was always a great deal of work to be done, always some pressing matter for attention. It was during a busy time that I called at the farm one Friday morning to check the latest intake of pigs for the stock register. As always, Mrs Lowe, whose Christian name I never knew, invited me in for a coffee and a sweet biscuit. As I settled at the rough kitchen table with the couple I noticed Shep asleep near the door which led into the back of the house. He ignored my presence.

After the introductory small talk and a brief chat about the quality of his latest acquisition of pigs, Ambrose asked:

"Does thoo reckon to know owt about dogs, Mr Rhea?"

"Not a great deal," I admitted.

"Oh," he said, without further comment.

"Something wrong?" I recognised the countryman's hesitation to lead into the problem. He wanted me to take the initiative, and turned his head to look down upon the sleeping dog.

"Aye, mebbe. Ah'm not sure."

"Something to do with Shep?"

"It could be his age," he said.

Mrs Lowe next spoke up. "He's twelve, you see, and he's had a hard life."

"Is he lame or something?" I ventured, thinking the dog might have a form of rheumatism.

"Nay, lad, nowt like that," and Ambrose paused to drink from his cup. "I reckon he's gone deaf."

"Deaf?"

"Aye, deaf. Dogs do go deaf, thoo knows, quite young sometimes. But awd Shep's getting on in years . . ."

"Has the vet seen him?"

"No, he hasn't, and Ah didn't feel like calling him all this way if it was nowt."

"He would tell you one way or the other," I said seriously. "And he might be able to treat the condition."

Mrs Lowe spoke again. "You see, Mr Rhea, we don't think he's really deaf. We think he's pretending."

"Pretending?" I almost laughed aloud. "Dogs can't pretend; they can't tell lies or be devious, can they?"

"Ah reckon thus 'un is, Mr Rhea," said Ambrose, who now seemed relieved that his wife had opened up the conversation by mentioning their private worry.

"You must have a good reason for thinking that," I put to them both.

"Aye, we 'ave, Mr Rhea," said Ambrose. "It's not a sudden idea, like. Me and our missus have been watching Shep of late, and Ah'm positive he's up to summat."

"Tell me more." I sipped from my cup.

"It's like this," he began carefully, speaking slowly with emphasis on the key words. "Ah've noticed, over t' past few weeks, that when Ah tell Shep it's time to start work, he just lies near yon door and never moves. We've both tried him . . ."

"Aye," confirmed Mrs Lowe. "Ah've told him it's time to fetch t' cows in, or round up a few sheep, and he just lies there, never twitching an eyelid. We've had to kick him into life, you know. Clout him with a mop or summat, and then he'll stir himself. Bone-idle he is."

"He could be deaf," I said. "If he's always been a good worker before . . ."

"Aye, lad," Ambrose raised a finger to emphasise the point, "but when oor missus tells him it's dinner-time, he hears that all right! By gum, he does that! He's up and at his dinner like a flash. We tried whispering, real quiet like, and he never missed a meal. Not once. But you try and tell him its milking time and he has to fetch t'cows in, and he'll doze there like it would take a bomb to shift him."

"He thinks it's time we got another dog, I reckon," Mrs Lowe offered her opinion. "I mean, in human terms, he's turned eighty, isn't he? He should be retired and he knows it."

"Let's see how he reacts now," I suggested. "Will he behave like that while I'm here?"

"He won't dare do otherwise if he doesn't want to be caught out!" and Ambrose Lowe put on a coat, took a crook from the corner and made all the noises he would have made under a normal excursion to locate sheep. Then he said, "Come, Shep, come lad."

I watched the inert form at the base of the door. The dog never moved, not even a flicker of an eyelid or a movement of an ear.

"Shep, come on, time to get sheep," called his master.
Nothing.

"It's a rum soort of a gahin on." I momentarily lapsed into the dialect of the area. "Is he allus like this?"

"Aye, just now. Now Ah'll get outside and pretend Ah've gone, leaving him there. Ooor missus will tell him it's dinner-time and thoo see what he does."

I waited as the little drama was acted out. Ambrose left the farmhouse and made the normal noises for such an occasion. Shep slept on. Then Mrs Lowe began to prepare a dog's dinner. She found his old enamel plate and opened the pantry door to produce some old bones and dog-biscuits from a tin. She placed these on the plate then put it on the floor, making a small noise. I saw Shep's ears prick at the sound.

"Come, Shep," she said in a normal voice. "Dinner."

And he was on his feet in a split second. Wagging his long tail, he moved quickly across the floor and began to wolf down his meal, showing sheer enjoyment and every sign of fitness.

This dog was certainly not deaf and he was most certainly not suffering from rheumatics. But could a dog feign deafness in order to avoid work? I doubted it. Surely dogs didn't possess that sort of cunning?

When he was midway through the meal, Ambrose returned and smiled at the active dog.

"Well?" he asked me.

I shook my head. "He heard Mrs Lowe all right. He must know when you're going out to work, eh? By the noises you make. He just lies there, waiting for you to call him, then ignores you . . ."

"He makes a good draught-excluder for yon door, and that's about all he's good for these days," commented Mrs Lowe. "What can we do, Mr Rhea? He's bone-idle — look at him. He's getting fatter all the time and more and more lazy."

I shook my head in bewilderment, then asked, "Have you come across this before, either of you? In other dogs — yours or anyone else's?"

"Never," he said firmly. "Never."

"A vet might have," I ventured. "Maybe if you rang the vet, he'd have a simple answer. It's maybe a common condition."

"Them fellers cost money, and Ah've enough trouble making ends meet as it is. Nay, I wanted a second opinion and you happened to come along. You've confirmed what we thought. So now, would you say he's having us on?"

"It looks very much like it." I didn't dare commit myself totally. How could I say, in all honesty, that this dog was nothing more than a confidence trickster or at least, one of the nation's shirkers?

I looked at Shep. He had finished his hefty meal and had returned to the space at the base of the inner door, where he lay down, sighed loudly and closed his eyes.

"It's milking time at half past four," Ambrose told me. "Ah'll warrant Ah'll nivver shift him then unless I clout him. By, he's takkin a lot of waking up these days."

I continued to watch the inert canine form and wondered if Shep could understand what we were saying. He gave no indication that he could hear us or understand us, and then an idea came to me.

"I've an idea," I said. "I think we could teach him a lesson!"

"Ah've yelled and cursed him, and we've both knocked him to his feet," said Ambrose. "Ah don't think there's owt a policeman can do."

"Why don't you both convince Shep that he really *is* deaf?" I suggested.

For a moment, there was no response from the couple, then Ambrose looked sideways at me. "How do you mean, Mr Rhea?"

"Well," I began, "I noticed that you made a lot of noise getting ready to go out. Banging doors, tapping your crook on the floor, that sort of thing. And your missus, well, she banged his plate down, there was a noise when she opened the pantry door and got the stuff out . . . and there's the words you use, like dinner, food, cows and so on. He knows what they all mean. He's a clever dog."

"Aye," agreed Ambrose.

"Well, whenever he's lying there, you should do everything very, very quietly. Make no noise at all. And if you talk to him when he's awake just shape the words, don't speak them. Put his dinner down silently and don't tell him it's ready . . . make him *think* he's gone deaf."

"By lad, that's a capper!" grinned Ambrose. "Aye, we can do that, can't we, oor missus?"

"It won't be easy, Mr Rhea, will it? I mean, he'll hear other noises, won't he, and we might forget sometimes . . ."

"I don't think it will take very long to get him puzzled about it," I ventured. "A day or two. It might cure his idleness."

"Right, we'll try it."

I hadn't time to remain behind on this occasion in order to see how this middle-aged rural couple went about their deception. Knowing the pair, it would have been a treat to observe them both mouthing silent words at each other and putting everything down in total silence when the dog was there — which was most of the time. When I told Mary about it, she laughed until the tears ran down her face, and said she thought I was crackers. I began to wonder who was daft — me or that lazy dog!

The Lowes weren't on the telephone so I couldn't ring them to ask about Shep's deafness cure, so I was delighted when I had to pop over to the farm later that week to see about a movement licence for some pigs.

I arrived at my usual time, just before eleven, and knew there'd be a cup of coffee and biscuits. Mrs Lowe saw me coming and, as I parked the motorcycle against a wall, she beckoned me to enter. She also placed a finger across her lips, indicating silence. She then came out to meet me, closing the outer door very, very quietly.

"By," she said, "our Shep's right puzzled."

"You're still giving him the treatment?" I exclaimed.

"We are," she confirmed. "Ambrose said we should keep it up until you came next time, so you could see if it worked. So here you are."

"It should be interesting," I smiled. "Where is Ambrose?"

"He'll be in any minute for his elevenses," she said. "Any road, he'll have heard your bike."

She took me into the kitchen where Shep lay in his usual place at the base of the door, performing his role as a draught-excluder and forgetting he was a working farm dog. As I entered, he looked quizzically at me, but Mrs Lowe smiled and mouthed the words, "Would you like a coffee?"

Feeling something of an idiot, I answered "Yes" in an exaggerated silence.

She went about the chore and I noted that she did everything in total silence. She had become expert at her new skill. The cups and saucers made not a sound, the kettle was boiled in the kitchen and everything was done completely without noise. Within five minutes, Ambrose entered and it was like watching a silent film. The couple went about their daily domestic chores in a remarkable way and I saw the puzzled dog watching this charade. He shook his head several times, and looked at me as if to ask what on earth was happening. Ambrose smiled, sat down and carried on a weird conversation with me, saying absolutely nothing and I responded in like manner. If Sergeant Blaketon came in now . . .

To complete the performance, Mrs Lowe got Shep's dinner ready. Out came a tin of dog-biscuits, some old bones and scraps, and a tin of dog-meat. His old enamel plate was placed on the floor in total silence and then she looked at him. He looked at her and shook his head, and she mouthed the words, "Come, Shep, dinner."

Shep looked at me and then at her, struggled heavily from his prone position and ambled across to eat the meal. As he licked the plate there was a faint noise as it scudded about the floor, but he appeared to ignore this. Then, having eaten, he returned to the door, curled up and lay down, but this time kept his large brown eyes open, watching us all in turn.

Ambrose smiled at me and mouthed the words, "Now, let's see if all this performance has fettled him."

Getting up from the chair, he went over to the crook in the corner, banged its ferrule on the floor and, in a normal voice, said, "Shep, come along. Time for work."

The dog lay there for the briefest of moments before leaping to his feet with a delighted bark. In no time, he was panting at the door wanting to be out. The ruse had worked perfectly. Or had it?

That weekend, in the Brewers Arms at Aidensfield, I heard Ambrose telling the tale to his drinking companions.

"By," he was saying, "oor dog was that glad he'd gat his hearing back, he ran inti my fields and rounded up all oor sheep and cows half a dozen times. He's never been idle since, Ah can tell you."

Nonetheless, I think Shep did win in the end. A few months later, Ambrose bought a young dog called Bob to take over from Shep, and Shep was honoured with the duty of showing the young dog how to work on the farm.

Before long, Shep would be officially retired. He'd earned his rest, and I knew that dog was far from stupid. But I did wonder what kind of tricks he would teach young Bob.

CHAPTER FOUR

Money is like muck, not good except it be spread.
FRANCIS BACON, 1561—1626

It has been said that if a ten-pence piece fell over the side of an ocean liner in a storm, the first man to reach the water after it would be a Yorkshireman and the second a Scotsman. The Jews are not in the race. It is difficult to assess the truth of this bold statement without actually testing it on location, but it is fair to say that where money is concerned a Yorkshireman does exercise considerable care.

Right across this massive county, the natives possess an inbred cunning where finance is involved and I think this yarn illustrates the point.

In a remote moorland village, the local simpleton found a half-crown lying in the middle of the road. This occurred in the days when a half-crown was of considerable value and the lad was delighted with his luck. It represented more than a day's wages. Off he went into the local pub to spend it and announced to the landlord that he wished to buy a pint of best bitter. The landlord, knowing the lad wasn't in the habit of spending his workaday pittance on beer, asked if he'd come into money.

"Aye," beamed the youth. "Ah've found a half-crown."

At this, a local ne'er-do'well approached the bar and said:

"Well, fancy that, Roger, that'll be that half-crown I lost this morning."

"Will it?" replied the finder sadly. "Did you lose it out there, in the street?"

"Aye, I did," agreed the trickster.

"And did your half-crown have a little hole drilled through it, just near t'date?"

"Aye, as a matter of fact it did!" smiled the villain of the piece.

"Well, this 'un hasn't," grinned the simpleton, handing it to the landlord.

Natural craftiness of this quality is perhaps the result of long and careful grooming in matters of finance, and there is little doubt that a close-fisted Yorkshireman is one of the meanest of creatures. He doesn't see it in that light, of course. He sees the issue as one of care coupled with necessity, and he does not believe in parting with his brass to anyone who hasn't earned it. It is no accident of history that a Yorkshireman's motto is:

Hear all, see all, say nowt,
Eat all, drink all, pay nowt,
And if thoo does owt for nowt,
Do it for thyself.

The county is replete with legendary yarns about the characteristic stinginess of Yorkshiremen and it is impossible to quote them all in these pages. To further illustrate Yorkshireman's niggardly attitude, the following parables are but examples.

There was a farmer's wife who sat beside her husband's deathbed, waiting for him to pass away. His customary meanness had infected her and it had been a long vigil. A candle burned at the bedside, for this was the only form of light in the house.

The long hours passed but the old man clung to life with all the grit and determination of his Yorkshire breeding. Then he turned to his wife and said, "I could use a nice cup o' tea, Martha."

"Nay, Sam," she said, "Ah'm not gahin to waste food on you now. Thoo mun do without. Thoo'll nut need food where thoo's gahin."

"But Ah's fair thosting for a drink," he said.

"Then Ah'll fetch a glass o'watter," and she rose from the bedside.

"Thanks," he managed to gasp in a sudden fit of coughing.

At this, she stopped at the door and said, "Sam, if thoo feels thysen slipping away while Ah'm downstairs, blow t' candle oot."

Another example occurred in our village post office before decimalisation came to harass the older folk. A local farmer entered to draw money from his Post Office Savings Account. The post-mistress produced the necessary forms and he completed them.

"Oh," she said when she read his words, "you can't draw out sixpence. You can only withdraw amounts of one shilling or greater." For those no longer familiar with £.s.d. money, a shilling was twelve old pennies, now worth 5p.

"I only want to buy six pennorth o' stamps," he retorted.

"I'm sorry, it'll have to be a shilling," she told him firmly and so he completed another form for that amount. He received his shilling, bought six pennyworth of post-age-stamps and then said, "Right missus, now I'd like to make a deposit."

"Certainly," she smiled. "How much?"

"Sixpence," he said and this time she had to accept his cash. There was no such rule about deposits.

Many local farmers and small business-people nurtured an open mistrust of banks. They utterly failed to understand the system and could never equate money with pieces of paper in cheque-books. Complicated matters like investments, securities, interest rates and the like were gibberish to these people, for they dealt always in cash, buying and selling everything in ready money and somehow managing to amass massive quantities of cash.

I have personally witnessed milk-churns full of old £5 notes, some of which had been there so long the money had gone green with damp and mould, and there is the classic tale of a son who tried to convert his old dad into depositing his money with a bank. After much explanation and pleading, the old man agreed to deposit £10,000 with the bank in town and he asked the son to fetch the milk-churn from the pantry.

They loaded the churn into the rear of the car and drove to the bank, where they manoeuvred this unusual purse into the building. There they stood and watched as the bewildered clerk counted out the money. Finally, she stopped.

"There's £9,997," she said, smiling at them.

At this, Dad turned to his son and grumbled, "Thoo silly young buffer, thoo's brought t'wrong churn!"

Then there was the miller who was eventually convinced that a bank account and a cheque-book was a good idea, and accordingly he deposited his £1000 with a local branch. After instruction from the manager, he went home with his brand new cheque-book and began to pay his bills. At the end of the month, the manager called him in and informed him that he was overdrawn.

"What's that mean?" asked the miller.

"It means you've overspent," explained the manager. "You've spent more than your £1,000."

"Don't be so daft!" retorted the miller. "I've never seen a penny of it!"

Knowing the true Yorkshireman's attitude to his money, it is interesting to spend time in one of the local markets, watching and listening to them as they wheel and deal among cattle, pigs, sheep and hens. Even today, there are many weekly markets in the small country towns of North Yorkshire, and it is traditional that the pubs are open all day for the service of suitable refreshment to those attending the market.

Attending market is one of a rural policeman's multifarious duties and, in my time, it was a regular task to attend for the sole purpose of issuing pig movement licences. These documents were vital if it was necessary to trace the movements of any pig thought to be affected by disease, and the farmers themselves knew and appreciated the value of this security. It was a simple system and it worked very well, both for the benefit of the police, the farmer, the vets and the Ministry of Agriculture.

The duty had many benefits, one of which was the pleasure of listening to the haggling that went on between farmers buying and selling. Even before they began, each knew the price he would either pay or receive, but, traditionally, there was, and still is, a great deal of good-natured haggling before reaching that figure. In addition, there is "luck money", a vital part of any deal.

A conversation might go something like this.

"How much for them pigs?"

"Fifteen quid apiece, and I'm letting you have 'em cheap."

"Fifteen quid? There's no such price for pigs! Nay, lad, thoo's not on wi' that sort of game."

"Fifteen or nowt. That's my price."

"I'll settle for ten."

"Ten? For these? Nivver. These are good pigs!"

"Ten is my figure and nut a penny more."

"By, thoo's a difficult chap ti deal with. These pigs is grand . . ."

"Twelve. Nea mair than twelve apiece."

"Push it up to twelve pound fifty and we might start talking."

"We'll talk when thoo comes down to eleven."

"Thoo just said twelve."

"Twelve was ti start thoo talking sense. Eleven apiece and that's my final offer."

"Twelve then, mak it twelve apiece."

"And luck money?"

"Aye, all right. A quid apiece for luck, then."

So he got them for £11 each. Such a deal can be a long-drawn-out affair, but luck money is always the concluding part of the deal and is always handed over in cash. It is not knocked off the price or added on. It is a cash transaction quite separate from the main deal, and marks the continuance of a very ancient custom in local cattle markets. Its origin is simply a method of bringing good luck to the transaction and the actual amount of money is a matter for negotiation. The conclusion of a deal, and the payment of luck money, is marked by the buyer and the seller slapping the palm of each other's hand. It is neither blackmail nor corruption, but a long-standing local custom that fills a few back pockets.

Such a purchase, with luck money, found me involved with one of Claude Jeremiah Greengrass's business enterprises. Most of his ventures concluded with my giving evidence against him in court, and I wondered if this was to be different.

It seemed that Claude Jeremiah had decided to enter the bacon business and he set about purchasing a dozen small pigs to make the foundations of his new enterprise. He knew that Joshua Sanders of Stang Farm, Maddleskirk, had a suitable litter for disposal and therefore went to see the dour farmer.

Joshua Sanders was noted as a hard and cunning businessman with a shrewd eye for a bargain but with a deep suspicion of those who never paid in cash. He disliked banks and, although he was now beginning to reluctantly accept cheques at the markets, he preferred to deal in ready money.

It must have been with some apprehension, therefore, that he opened his front door one Friday morning to find the notorious Claude Jeremiah Greengrass on the doorstep. Everyone knew of Claude's reputation as a small-time crook; he was untrustworthy, shady and should always be treated with caution. Joshua faced his potential customer with true Yorkshire grit.

"Noo then, Claude Jeremiah," greeted Joshua blandly.

"Good-morning, Mr Sanders." Claude smiled at the big man, his tiny pinched brown face wrinkled in the morning sun. "I hear tell you've a litter of pigs for sale."

"That might be right." Joshua was exercising his traditional caution. "There again, it might not. Who wants to know?"

"Me. I'm after buying some pigs," beamed the little man. "I'm getting established in the pig-breeding business, you see, and I need some good stock. Bacon's always a good investment."

"Well, now then." Joshua rubbed his bristly chin. "That's a capper," he was flummoxed for a moment or two. "Ah've more or less promised yon litter to a bloke from t'far side of Thirsk. Ah daren't let him down . . ."

Joshua was stalling. There were two reasons why he didn't want Claude Jeremiah to have these animals. One — he probably wouldn't pay for them, and two, if this was one of Claude Jeremiah's enterprises, everything connected with it would go wrong. The miserable little pigs would probably die from neglect and starvation . . .

"I can pay good money for them . . ." began the little man, pulling out his wallet. It was full of personal papers, and a cheque-book lay inside. "I've a bank account."

Knowing Joshua as I did, I guessed his brain was working very rapidly at this stage, desperately seeking some cast-iron reason for not selling his stock to Claude Jeremiah. But Claude Jeremiah was also cunning.

"Ah allus deals in cash," Joshua said by way of dismissing the nuisance.

"I've an old aunt in Australia who's left me a large amount of money," announced Claude Jeremiah. "She always wanted me to enter a business of some kind, and I've now got enough money to stand any loss I might make during the first couple of years. I want to employ a man to help me, and I intend to learn all about pigs."

"Old aunt?" Joshua's eyes opened wide at this revelation.

"Yes, on my mother's side. Aunt Jemima. You'll have seen her about the place, Mr Sanders. She's a tall woman with a bun at the back of her head, always voted Liberal and kept Yorkshire terriers. Loaded, she was. She went to live in Australia about nine or ten years ago . . . bought a sheep-ranch out there and made thousands. Well, she died and I've inherited a share of her money. I know you'll keep this to yourself, but I got over £15,000. Naturally, I want to put the money to good use . . . I've had sties built at my place and need some good stock to start my enterprise . . ."

Claude Jeremiah's well-rehearsed yarn would not have tempted a city businessman, but, in spite of his caution and in spite of his knowledge of Claude Jeremiah's past, this talk of wills, big money, faraway places and deceased aunts weakened the resolve of Joshua Sanders. But it was not completely weakened — that was impossible.

"Well, now young man," he said gently. "We might have a deal. If thoo reckons my pigs is good enough for you, and thoo pays a bigger price than that other chap was reckoning on, thoo can 'ave 'em."

Claude Jeremiah's pinched face broke into a happy smile.

"Come, Ah'll show thoo yon litter," offered the farmer.

It seems that Claude Jeremiah was highly impressed by the pink piglets as they ran and grunted about their large cosy home in a dry building. Accordingly, the traditional bidding began.

"Ah can't take less than £12 apiece," Joshua leaned on the gate and solemnly shook his head.

"I was thinking more on the lines of £8," came in Claude Jeremiah.

"There's no such price for decent pigs, not like these," and Joshua made as if to leave the building.

"Nine?"

"Mr Greengrass, thoo's very near insulting me with offers like that. £9 for these pigs? Nay, lad, thoo'll have to think harder than that. Thoo'd better try Aud Yeoman rather than me. His scrawny animals might fit that price."

71

"His pigs die after eight or nine weeks," said Claude Jeremiah. "He's got the kiss of death on pigs, has that chap."

"Well, that's the sort of pig thoo can expect with an offer like this. Nine quid a pig! Ah've never heard sike rubbish."

"Ten, then?"

Joshua rubbed his bristly chin once more.

"Mak it eleven and we'll begin talking."

"That's a lot of money for a chap to find for starters, Mr Sanders. What about me taking just half a dozen then? That would be £66 . . ."

"Nut a chance. It's all or nowt. A dozen or nowt, Claude Jeremiah. Twelve quid apiece."

"Tak eleven pounds ten bob each?" he queried.

Joshua leaned on the gate and pulled a large briar pipe from his jacket pocket. He began to poke and prod it and eventually lit the fearsome machine to produce clouds of sweet-smelling smoke.

"Ah'll tak eleven pund ten bob apiece then, on one condition."

"Condition?" Claude's eyes beamed with satisfaction but seconds later changed to a hue which indicated suspicion. Joshua was up to summat.

"Aye. At that price, thoo sees, Ah's letting them pigs go for next to nowt. It's a giveaway price."

"It's a fair price, Mr Sanders. The market price isn't as high as that. You can get good store pigs for £10 each . . ."

"But not of this quality, young man, not of this quality," and he waved the pipe around like a conductor's baton as if to emphasise his claims.

"What's this condition then?" asked Claude Jeremiah, cautiously.

Before announcing the condition which he was to impose upon Claude Jeremiah, Joshua had recognised the little man's anxiety to buy the pigs; he'd also taken account of his reputation as a confidence man and concluded that the tale about Aunt Jemima's fortune did not sound true. Joshua therefore needed some kind of surety, for he knew Claude would try to dodge paying cash. It was to be a dreaded cheque transaction.

"Well." Joshua puffed at the pipe. "Ah've an awd donkey down them fields. Nice friendly donkey, it is, used at the seaside for giving kids rides before it came out here to retire."

"Yes?"

"If thoo wants them pigs at eleven and a half quid apiece, thoo'll have to buy yon donkey an' all."

"But I don't want a donkey . . ."

"And Ah don't want to sell them pigs at £11 10s 0d apiece."

"What would I do with a donkey?" asked Claude Jeremiah.

"Sell it, mebbe, in time."

"What sort of price were you thinking for the donkey then?"

Joshua pursed his lips. "A giveaway price really, fifty quid."

"Fifty!"

"Aye."

"Look, Mr Sanders, I don't want a donkey . . ."

"But thoo dis want twelve good pigs, for a knockdown, giveaway price . . . them's my terms, Mr Claude Jeremiah Greengrass. And cash for t'donkey."

"Now look, I can't find that amount of money . . ."

"Then thoo dissn't get my pigs."

A long silence then descended as Claude Jeremiah gave this proposal his most earnest consideration.

"Forty," he said. "Cash, for t'donkey."

"Forty-five," countered Joshua.

"Right, £45 for the donkey, cash. And a cheque for the pigs?"

"Twelve pigs at £11 10s 0d each. That'll be £138," said Joshua like lightning, puffing at his pipe.

Out came Claude Jeremiah's cheque-book and he wrote a cheque for that amount. Then he delved into an inner pocket of his old coat, well away from his wallet, and surreptitiously produced £45 in notes, which he passed to the waiting farmer.

"What about my luck money?" asked Joshua.

That cost Claude Jeremiah another £5, cash.

"Right," said Joshua. "Thoo can take them pigs when thoo's ready, but t'donkey stays here."

"Stays here?" cried Claude Jeremiah.

"Aye, until that cheque gets through yon bank. That story aboot a rich aunt dissn't seem true ti me, so yon donkey stays put until that cheque is paid inti my bank."

"But you can't do that . . ."

"Ah just have," grinned Joshua. "Good-morning, Mr Greengrass."

Claude Jeremiah returned later in the day with a cattle-truck and loaded the twelve pigs. Joshua however had been active during Claude's absence. Realising that Claude might not take them home, but might instead sell them immediately for a profit, he had effectively prevented this by charging a very high price. Claude would have to keep them for a month or two in order to make any profit, upon his payment for the donkey, but just in case the cheque did bounce Joshua rang all the dealers that afternoon to warn them that the Greengrass pigs had been vomiting and seemed to have diarrhoea. That was enough to put any farmer off a deal; swine-fever was the last thing they wanted on their premises.

The outcome was that Claude was compelled to keep the pigs for a month or so, whether he liked it or not, and meanwhile the donkey remained on Joshua's farm.

As Joshua had anticipated, a week after the deal the cheque bounced. There were no funds. It had been a confidence trick after all and, when this became known, I was called in.

Mr Sanders invited me to join him in a large whisky and a slice of gingerbread as he explained how he'd been conned into parting with £138 worth of pigs for a worthless cheque. I was not told of the donkey at that stage. So far as I knew therefore, I had a case of false pretences on my hands, and a ready-made suspect for the crime.

"Ah doesn't want this to go to court," said Sanders when he'd finished his tale.

"Hang on, Mr Sanders," I said. "If you report this to me on an official basis, I'll have to take Claude Jeremiah to court. He's committed a criminal offence."

"But if Ah *knew* he'd try it on, and took steps to deal with it myself, Ah've not been conned, eh?"

"Er, no," I had to admit.

He then told me about the donkey deal and I laughed at the notion. I wondered who'd conned who — Claude had unwittingly paid for the pigs at a moderate price.

"So what do you want me to do?"

"See him and put the wind up him," said Joshua.

"That'll do no good!" I laughed. "Claude Jeremiah's my one regular court attender. He knows more about dealing with the court than anyone I know. You'll not put the wind up him."

"Well, Ah thought you might do summat, just to cap him."

"Come on, Mr Sanders. You've got something up your sleeve. What is it?"

"Well, Ah sees it like this. He's not paid for them pigs, so that makes 'em still mine. Right?"

"It might need a civil court action to definitely state that," I told him.

"Nay, be damned," he growled, "Ah'll not have that. Them's my pigs, Mr Rhea, and mak no mistake about it."

"So what's your plan?"

"Tell him you know about his dud cheque, tell him he might go to court for false pretences or whatever you said it was, and then give him another month to pay me. Cash."

"He'll never pay you! You shouldn't have sold him those pigs!"

"But you'll do that, for me, eh?"

"It might get him off the hook, and I'll forget about the donkey?"

"Aye, for now."

Claude Jeremiah Greengrass had won so many battles against me and my colleagues that I felt justified in going along with Joshua's little scheme. After all, if he had not been deceived in any way by Claude Jeremiah's stories, the episode was nothing more than a bad business transaction and therefore of no interest to the police. So I went along to Claude's home and told him what I knew.

From the little man, I got a tale of woe and sorrow. He told me how he'd bought the pigs knowing of a ready market for them, but old Joshua had stopped all that by telling everybody for miles around that there was summat wrong with the animals. And no one would pay the price he'd paid.

"So, Mr Rhea, I can't sell the pigs to get my money back. If I'd sold them straight away, I'd have made enough to pay Mr Sanders and a little bit for me on the donkey deal."

"Claude Jeremiah," I said. "I know you too well. You would have made a profit, but kept the lot for yourself and you never would have paid Sanders. I know that, and he knows that. But he's made a very generous offer — he'll allow you one month to pay. You've a month to make £138 and square up with him. Otherwise it's court for you."

"A month? I'll never make that sort of cash in a month, Mr Rhea, besides, he's got my donkey."

"If you choose to let your donkey graze on his land, that's a private deal between yourselves," I dismissed the problem.

I left Claude Jeremiah to his worries and told Sanders what I'd done. He smiled and asked me to go and visit the farm in a month's time. I made a note in my diary.

A month later to the day, I made the bumpy journey to Stang Farm and found Joshua in the stackyard, smoking his pipe.

"Ah heard yon bike coming up our lane," he said. "It'll be about Greengrass, eh?"

"Has he paid?" I asked.

"Not a penny. I knew he wouldn't. Right, Mr Rhea, my cattle-truck's ready. Let's go."

"Go where?" I cried.

"Greengrass's place, to pick up my pigs."

"You're retrieving them?"

"Aye, they're still my pigs. You'll be needed to prevent a breach of the peace, I reckon."

And so I followed his rickety old vehicle down to the Greengrass abode and there we confronted the little man. He had no money; he had been cleaned out of cash by Sanders' actions in selling him the donkey, and his expenses on food had not allowed him to make up the deficit. So the pigs were herded squealing and protecting into the cattle-truck and Sanders smiled at me.

"There'll be no court case, Mr Rhea?"

"Not on this occasion," I smiled.

"What about the cost of feeding those pigs?" asked Claude Jeremiah before we left. "I've had your twelve pigs on my premises for over a month, and I've fed them all that time . . ."

"And they look very well on it," smiled Joshua.

"You'll pay me the going rate for boarding them?"

"That just equals the rent of that field of mine where you graze your donkey," smiled Joshua. "I reckon we're square."

"But you've had a month's free accommodation for those pigs!" came in Claude Jeremiah. "You can't do that."

"Ah've just done it," grinned Joshua. "Call for your donkey when you can. The rental goes up next week. If you can't pay, I could always sell the donkey to settle your overdue account."

And off he drove, very happy with himself.

Claude Jeremiah Greengrass looked miserable in the extreme. He'd been beaten by this crafty old farmer and I was delighted.

"You wouldn't like to buy a nice donkey, Mr Rhea?" asked Claude Jeremiah as I climbed aboard my motorcycle.

"From you? It might have epizootic lymphangitis!" I laughed as I rode into the sunshine. I left the little man with a very puzzled frown on his weathered features and learned later that it was impossible to catch that donkey. It had lived for years in that field, defying all attempts to get it into a halter or a vehicle.

"If anybody can catch yon donkey, Mr Rhea," smiled Joshua a week later, "They can have it."

* * *

It could be said that police officers are the dustmen of society, many of them spending their days cleaning up the offal left by the baser forms of humanity. It is true they do spend a lot of man-hours dealing with matters that no one else would cope with, even if they were ordered to. Happily, there is a list of things which must not be done by policemen in the course of their duties and this includes the collection and recovery of money under affiliation orders, the collection and recovery of money under maintenance orders (except the acceptance of monies paid to a police station) the collection of market tolls, the duties of mayor's attendant, or town-crier, the regular cleaning of police-stations when the Home Secretary has directed that it is not a police duty, and any other work not connected with police duty which the Home Secretary decides is not to be performed by the police.

Strangely, we are allowed to perform a weird range of other duties, like enforcing cinematograph acts and regulations and borough byelaws; then there are billeting duties, the inspection of domestic servants' registries, common lodging-houses, hackney carriages, licensed boats, beach trading, markets, fire appliances and street lamps, and we may also issue pedlars' certificates.

In addition, there are diseases of animals, licensing matters, duties under the Shops Act and a host of other miscellaneous odds and sods that no one else seems anxious to do. So the police have to do all these things, as well as fight crime, keep traffic flowing, and battle with pickets, demonstrators and yobbos.

It is difficult to specify the most unsavoury of our duties, but for my mind the execution of a distress warrant is one of the worst. This document was not uncommon in underprivileged urban areas but I scarcely expected to be faced with one during my spell in rural Aidensfield.

It was with some interest therefore that I answered the call to attend Ashfordly Police Station one fine morning for a chat with Sergeant Bairstow. When he spoke on the telephone, he gave no indication of the turmoil that was to come, but I should have realised it would be something very complicated. He loved giving me the awkward jobs.

"Ah, Nick," he said as I walked in, removing my helmet with a flourish.

"Good-morning, Sarge." I used the diminutive of his rank, an indication of my progress on the beat. I might even be allowed to refer to him by his Christian name during off-duty moments — only time would tell.

"Nick," he said smiling with what I discovered was an evil grin. "I've a nice little job for you."

"Something special?" I wondered if I had to interview the Lady of the Manor, or talk to a lovely girl about something fascinating. Maybe, he'd solved a crime and wanted me to arrest the suspect . . .

"Yes," he said as he lifted a file from the desk. "A distress warrant. We've got one to execute in Crampton."

"A distress warrant?" I opened my mouth with astonishment. "Here?"

"Yes, here," he said, showing me the document in question.

Every warrant is a directive signed by a magistrate, and the policeman must read it with a view to learning what his duty is to be. This one said that the Police in Ashfordly must distrain goods to the value of £107 15s 8d because of the non-payment of rates by a Mr Charles Edward Hatfield of The Bungalow, Church Lane, Crampton.

I read it carefully, scarcely believing my eyes. I had no idea these things were actually issued; we had been told about them at Training School and we had been given a good grounding about the problems and routine of executing them. It was rather like learning about Henry VIII or

Napoleon — we knew they had existed but never expected to meet them.

But this document was real enough, and it was signed by Alderman Fazakerly to give it authenticity.

"What shall I do with it, Sergeant?" I reverted to the formal mode of address.

"You will deal with it," he smiled wickedly.

I studied the terrifying piece of paper for a long time, wondering how I would cope. Charlie Bairstow watched me and I knew my hesitancy was amusing him, but I was determined not to allow him better me this time. I'd had enough of his pranks with zebras, ghosts and the like. This was a real job.

"I must get the money out of him," I said. "Otherwise we seize goods to the value of £107 15s 8d."

"He won't pay up, he never does," came the reply.

"He's a regular?" I asked.

"One of the regulars, perhaps *the* most regular of the regulars," Charlie Bairstow told me. "Mr Hatfield never pays his rates. The Council always send people around, they cajole him and bully him, but he never pays. Then we get lumbered with a distress warrant to seize goods to the value of the outstanding amount."

"I'll need more than the stated amount, won't I?"

"Yes, much more. You must arrange to sell the seized goods at a local auction, leaving enough profit to pay expenses and to ensure there's enough to pay off the rates."

"I might frighten him into paying cash?"

"You might," he laughed.

Tucking the offensive piece of paper in my pocket, I sallied from the office and journeyed over to Crampton, about six miles away. I had never encountered Mr Charles Edward Hatfield and wondered what kind of person could leave his rate payments so that they accumulated into impossible amounts.

I soon found out.

Before actually knocking on his door, however, I popped into my own office to swot up the rules and procedures on distress warrants. My memory did not produce the precise rules, and I knew my notes taken at Training School would guide me.

Certain items had not to be seized when I swooped on The Bungalow; they were the wearing apparel or the bedding of the person and his family, and I was not allowed to seize the implements of his trade to the value of £5. This was to allow the fellow to continue to earn. I was not allowed to seize goods which he did not own or which were the subject of hire-purchase agreements and rentals. I could not break into the house to carry out this duty, and I had not to raid him during the night hours. All this was coming home to me now; my training had been sound.

I had to mark the seized goods in a manner which was clear and conspicuous; this was for the benefit of the removal men when they arrived in due course, and it was an offence for the householder to delete my marks. I decided the best way was to take a pile of sticky labels and fix these to the seized items, endorsing each one with my signature.

Having marked all the goods, I had then to leave them in the house until I could arrange a sale. This meant contacting the local auction room on the understanding that the sale had to take place not earlier than the sixth nor later than the fourteenth day after I had marked the goods, unless the householder agreed in writing to an earlier sale. I knew the saleroom at Ashfordly held weekly sales on a Friday, so that seemed not to present problems.

If the fellow had no goods, or there were insufficient to cover the costs, I had to endorse the warrant and return it to the Justices' Clerk. That seemed simple enough. What the Clerk did thereafter was not my problem, I hoped.

Armed with this useful information, I continued my journey to Crampton and parked my motorcycle in Church Lane. The Bungalow was not difficult to find.

It was a rickety construction of dark green hue, comprising timber and corrugated-iron sheets rusting about the metal edges and needing a coat of paint upon the wooden bits. A short red-brick chimney protruded from the roof and clouds of black smoke were belching from it. The smoke rose straight into the sky, which, to my countryman's eye, indicated a fine day tomorrow. All the windows were closed and needed cleaning, while the garden resembled a rough shoot or a haven for harassed weeds. An untidy thorn hedge bordered the premises and there was a little wooden gate leading into the grounds. A rough path led through the weeds to a rustic porch with honeysuckle climbing about it. It was picturesque in a grotty sort of way.

I let myself in, marched along the path with the determination of a constable under orders and knocked on the battered old door. I could hear movements inside and eventually a scruffy man with a grey beard revealed himself.

"Mr Hatfield?" I asked.

"That's me, son," he smiled through the untidy mop of hair.

"P.C. Rhea," I introduced myself. "From Aidensfield."

"Aye, I guessed as much. You'll have come with one of those distress warrants, I'll guess."

"I have, yes. It's for a large amount, non-payment of your rates . . ."

"Come in, son. We'll talk about it. I don't believe in paying rates. Would you, for a spot like this? I know it's my home, and I know it's falling down, but rates? I never use the library, I don't send kids to school, I never drive a car along the roads, I don't spend any of the ratepayers' money, so why should I pay rates, Mr Rhea? Answer me that."

By now, we were inside and it was dark and dingy. There was no one else in the house and he led me towards a wooden table with a dirty top overflowing with cups and milk-bottles.

"Cup of tea?" he invited.

"No thanks, I've just had one," I lied. I couldn't face drinking from one of those cups. The whole place was filthy and almost devoid of furniture.

"How much is it?" he asked.

"One hundred and seven pounds, fifteen shillings and eight pence," I informed him, reading from the warrant.

"That's accumulated over four or five years," he smiled. "They don't know what to do with me. They daren't put me in prison. Every year, I get my rate demands and every year I fail to pay. Then, every year, the bobby calls with one of those bits of paper and tells me I'll be for it if I don't cough up. But I never do, Mr Rhea. Have a look around. What can you take? Clothing, no. Bedding, no. Implements of my trade? I have none. That table? It's my sister's — she loans it to me. Cups and saucers, pots and pans — they're hers. You can't take them. My radio and television — I rent them. I've nothing, Mr Rhea."

"You haven't a job?"

"Not me! Why work? I can get money from the State, enough to feed me and keep me warm. Why work, eh? Look at you, doing a job like this. You can't like it . . ."

"I don't, not this sort of thing."

"Then why do it? Why not live every day as if there's no tomorrow, eh?"

"I couldn't . . ." I found myself beginning a discussion with him and knew I'd lose. You can't argue with folks of fixed opinions and it was clear to me that this character had very fixed views on life. "Look, Mr Hatfield, I'm here to seize goods in this house to the value of the warrant. May I now look around?"

He indicated the living-room door and I walked in. It was almost bare. The floor was uncovered, showing bare sandstone with a worn rug upon the area in front of the empty fireplace. A battered old armchair occupied a corner — in a sale it might fetch five shillings. And that was all, except for the television and the radio in the corner near the window.

"Rented," he said, shoving his hand under the TV set. He pulled out a rental agreement for each item and I had to agree. I could not seize those.

"Bedroom?" he asked me.

I nodded and he showed me into a small room at the rear. There was a single bed neatly made and covered with a faded eiderdown. Beside it stood a cane chair painted blue, while a wardrobe had been built into one wall. I opened it; it contained his clothes, such as they were. There was not even a chest of drawers. Next to the bedroom there was a crude bathroom albeit with an electric heater for the water and a water-closet.

And that was it. My seizures were:- living-room, nil; kitchen, nil; bathroom and bedroom, nil.

"Nothing, Mr Rhea, like I said," and he smiled wickedly at me. I knew I was beaten. How long would the Council tolerate this, I wondered? He might be threatened with imprisonment if he failed to pay this time.

"Look," I tried to be firm. "It'll mean prison for you, Mr Hatfield. You can't keep on like this for ever. The Council has been very, very tolerant with you . . ."

"I wrote to 'em, a long time ago, Mr Rhea, and suggested they send me to prison. I'd be fed and clothed in there, eh? And I still wouldn't pay my rates."

"Why have you stopped paying them?" I decided to ask. "You must have paid until four or five years ago."

"I did, young man, and was pleased to pay my way. But it's these scroungers, you know, folks who live off those who are daft enough to work and pay taxes. Well, I couldn't see why an old man like me should have to pay for idle sods who can't be bothered to earn their keep. So I stopped my rates, a form of protest, you see."

"If everybody stopped, Mr Hatfield, there'd be no education for the kids, no roads, no future for anyone."

"Get the scroungers back to work and I'll pay up," he said with an air of finality.

"I'll call back tomorrow," I said. "I'll expect the cash. I can't accept cheques."

"There'll be nowt for you, young man. Sorry. It'll be a wasted journey."

He was right, but I had to go through the motions of exhausting every possibility. Besides, Sergeant Bairstow would want me to account for my actions, and he'd want money.

While I was in Crampton, I decided to undertake a short foot patrol about the village and was soon chatting to the locals over garden walls, in house doorways and in the street. This was rural policing at its best — a friendly type of person willing and happy to pass the time of day. with the local bobby. And it was an old man who hailed me from his greenhouse.

"Here, Bobby, come and see this," he beckoned.

I let myself into his neat garden and entered the well-kept greenhouse. It was full of cacti; large and small, plain and decorative, and he pointed to one with a huge red flower at the end of a thick stem.

"How about that?" he beamed.

"Very, very nice," I enthused. "Did you grow it?"

"I did," he said proudly. "And do you realise it flowers only once every seven years. And this is it. Seven years and she's flowering today, my birthday, would you believe. By, I am capped."

He then told me all about cacti and quoted lots of weird foreign names. He kept me there nearly half an hour but I enjoyed his prattle. Finally he said, "My missus will have a kettle on. Come and have a cup."

I learned his name was Albert Peacock and we had a very enjoyable cup of tea and a chat.

"Now then," he said after I'd met his wife, drunk his tea and looked at more cacti on his window-ledges, "I asked you in for a reason."

"Trouble?" I asked.

"Nay," he said, "but I seed you up at old Hatfield's spot."

"Yes, I called just now," I confirmed.

"Rates, again, I'll bet. The old sod never pays, you know, and you fellers keep coming with warrants. We know what he's like, and the village reckon it's time he was made to pay. We all pay up."

"There's very little anyone can do," I said. "He has nothing to sell . . ."

"He's worth thousands," said Albert. "Mebbe tens of thousands. He's got money all over, because he never pays for owt. He's the tightest bloke I've come across, is yon."

"Is he? His place looks terrible . . ."

"It is terrible because he neglects it, and won't pay for a tin o' paint or tools to fettle his garden with. He'll tell you a load of rubbish about spongers, but that's all tommy-rot."

"I can't raid his bank account," I smiled.

"Nay, but you can raid his loft," he nodded knowingly.

"Loft?"

"You didn't see it?"

"There's no door into a loft in that cottage," I said.

"There is, thoo knows," he winked. "In t'bedroom, far corner. Loose boards, they are, looking just like the others in the ceiling. No handles, nor nowt. Just a flat board sitting in place. Push it up and a ladder'll come down, folding down over."

"How do you know this?"

"Late one night, I thought I heard somebody in my garden, so I crept out. Well gone midnight, it was, and I saw a light in Hatfield's spot. So, being nosey, I had a look and saw him climbing up. He hadn't drawn his curtains, 'cos he hasn't any."

"And what's up there?" I put the obvious question.

"Paintings," he said. "Lots of paintings."

"Valuable ones?"

"They'll be valuable, or he wouldn't have 'em," said Albert. "Then I saw him one day at a sale, buying up all the old oils and watercolours."

"Thanks, Mr Peacock," I smiled.

"No saying how you knew, eh?"

"Not a word," I promised.

I went back immediately.

He answered the door and was clearly surprised to see me so soon.

"Hello, Mr Hatfield," I beamed. "I just got down to the bottom of the village when I realised I hadn't looked in your loft."

"Loft?" he blanched.

"Yes, looking at your cottage from down the village, there's clearly a loft. I wondered if you had anything up there that we might sell to raise the money."

I could see his mind working. For a person who collects or hoards, money is of less value than the goods in question, and I knew his brain was working rapidly.

"You said you'd call back tomorrow?" he put to me.

"I did."

"Will you do that then? It won't be a wasted journey this time. How much is it?"

I told him once again and emphasised that I must be given cash, for on occasions of this kind cheques were not acceptable.

"I'll have it ready," he said frowning. "You won't want to be in my loft, will you?"

"Not if the money is available tomorrow at this time," I told him.

I called again as promised and it was there, in cash, down to the last penny. I endorsed the warrant in his presence. This effectively killed the document and I issued him with a receipt.

The formalities over, I smiled.

"I might see you next year, Mr Hatfield?"

"I'll have the cash ready," he said, "but I might give them a run for their money, like this time."

"I don't mind the trip," I said.

Afterwards, I wondered what kind of pictures he had collected and I speculated upon their value. But it seemed I would never know the answer.

But I reckoned that Charlie Hatfield would pay his rates so long as I was the village bobby.

"Did he pay?" smiled Sergeant Bairstow, but the smile vanished as I produced the cash and the endorsed warrant.

"How did you manage that?" he asked.

"By causing a little distress," I said.

# CHAPTER FIVE

What a pity it is that we have no amusements
in England but vice and religion.
REV. SIDNEY SMITH, 1771—1845

When the Reformation swept the valleys and moors of
the North Riding of Yorkshire, it missed one or two areas.
These became known as hotbeds of Papists or Centres of
Catholicism, depending upon which God you worshipped.
The statutory new Anglican religion did its best to fill the
pews wrested from the Catholics but in the passage of time
this failed. Anglican churches are emptying as the Catholic
are refilling. Wesley had to go too; he tried to reform the
reformed and his efforts produced a crop of chapels right
across the hills, many of them nestling in remote places to
echo with the voices of song-happy dalesmen.

Eventually they too began to lose their fervour. History
repeated itself and the Catholics returned to build new
churches. They built a monastery at Maddleskirk and monas-
ticism returned to the dales. As time went by, the old religious
wounds were healed and the various faiths mixed in business, in
pleasure and in matrimony, but seldom in church. Inevitably,
a little of the old misunderstanding and antagonism remained,

so the Catholics went to Mass in their churches or abbeys, the Anglicans attended services in their ancient places and the Methodists went to chapel and sang with great gusto. The many other little faiths did their stuff too. Everyone seemed content.

No one made any real attempt to understand the other's point of view, all believing God was of their faith, but as the second half of the twentieth century entered the history-books there did appear a softening of attitudes. The new movement became known as ecumenism which really meant Catholics could attend services in Protestant churches, and Protestants could join Catholics in prayer. Real and sincere efforts were made by those in charge of the various religions and places of worship, and it was pleasing to see all faiths joined together in prayer on occasions like Armistice Day or the induction of vicars or welcoming of priests.

While all this ecumenical chat was being encouraged by religious leaders, no one bothered to tell those of their faith who seldom attended church. Those in the happy circle knew all about ecumenism, but that great mass of the public who didn't go to church were not informed about the new developments. Many stalwart members of every faith therefore steadfastly refused to bend their opinions, and this caused me something of a problem at a local funeral.

My official role in the affair was that of traffic policeman. The deceased, a man called James Bathurst, was well known around Elsinby and Aidensfield, having served on the parish council, the county council, the Police Standing Joint Committee and the parochial church council. A widower of seven or eight years, Mr Bathurst had lived alone in a lovely house which had been his family home for generations.

There had been Bathursts in Elsinby for hundreds of years, proof of which was very evident upon the gravestones and upon the various rolls of honour affixed to the sturdy walls of the parish church. The family was Anglican through and through; Bathursts had supported the church in all its troubles, donating pews, stained-glass windows, altar-cloths and many other things as and when necessary. Verily, they had been a marvellous family and generous benefactors.

I did not get to know James Bathurst very well, for he died soon after my arrival at Aidensfield. I did know, however, that he had not been in very sound health for some months and that he had been more or less confined to his house. A lady from the village went in daily to feed him and clean the premises, and it seems he had had a very pleasant and fulfilled life.

The one problem was that he never produced an heir, male or female. This meant he was the last of the Bathursts, for he was an only son. Finally, therefore, the Bathurst dynasty ended and I was privileged to direct traffic at the funeral of the very last member. I was present during a moment of local history.

Money for the funeral came from the provisions of his last will and testament, and the house was to be sold by auction. I knew all this and I was told by his solicitor that the funeral would be a massive affair. It was he who requested my presence to ensure that the hearse got to the church, that the mourners found parking-places and that the passing traffic flowed freely on its way. I agreed, for this was part of my duty as the village constable.

What I did not realise was that Mr James Bathurst had upset Elsinby and district in such a way that many of the residents felt deeply snubbed and very hurt. On his deathbed, he had decided to join the Roman Catholic church.

Some local Anglicans, distant relations and other interested bodies were later to attempt to contest his will because he had decreed that he be buried within the grounds of the little R.C. church of St Francis of Assisi, and that the proceeds from the sale of his house and other belongings be given to various Catholic charities.

In the days before the funeral, I learned of the various rippling undercurrents but felt such problems were not my concern. My sole duty was to attend the funeral and ensure the smooth flow of traffic and easy passage of people.

In spite of parish mutterings, the funeral was fixed for 2 p.m. one Saturday in April at the Catholic Church of St Francis of Assisi at Elsinby. It is a pretty little church with a neat graveyard nearby and is almost opposite the Anglican parish church. I visited the locality before the funeral, making my decisions about who should park where, and what to do with the hearse. There was plenty of room; I could foresee no problems.

In spite of the parochial upset, a large crowd comprising faithful of all denominations was anticipated, along with various dignitaries from the organisations he had supported. The Catholics, of course, were cock-a-hoop with pride that such a noted person had joined them albeit in the final moments of his long life. They totally rejected the suggestion that he had become a Catholic simply to prevent the death of an Anglican. And, being a Catholic myself, I was also pleased about it, and knew dear old James would find peace in the long silence that was to come. It was Abraham Cowley who said, "An eternal now does always last."

At 1.15 p.m., therefore, I positioned myself outside the church and was vaguely aware of the grave-digger, old Dusty Miller, wandering into the pub with a shovel over his shoulder. He had completed his part in the event. Minutes later, the mourners began to arrive, all wanting a front seat as Father Brendan O'Malley watched over them. Suddenly, I was busy. I parked cars, bade "good afternoon" to lots of solemn folk and ushered them all into the tiny church which soon boasted standing room only.

The coffin and its contents were already inside, having been previously brought into the building. The hearse had long since gone, for the graveyard lay just behind the church. James would be speeded to his eternal rest with the full splendour of a Requiem Mass, intoned by a priest in black vestments. It was truly a moving occasion, and even some hardened atheists, Methodists and Anglicans were moved to tears by the Irish eloquence of Father O'Malley's tribute to the deceased. In the Latin parts of the Mass, he spoke with rare feeling and, even though the Latin was incomprehensible to most of those present, it sounded fine and noble.

Then came the interment. Six powerful lads of Elsinby, dressed in sombre black, prepared to carry the coffin to the grave. Seated at the back, I made my move — I hurried outside to ensure the little gate was open, and found the undertaker looking somewhat harassed.

"Mr Rhea," he breathed in sepulchral tones. "There's no grave!"

"No grave?" I cried.

"No," he said. "I've been right round the churchyard, looking for somewhere to put the flowers, but there's no grave. They haven't dug one . . ."

"But I saw Dusty Miller with his spade . . ." I cried.

"They're coming . . ." and he galloped into the graveyard once more to make a final search. I didn't know whether to tell Father O'Malley or not; after all, the undertaker might have been mistaken. So I decided to let the procession pass.

With Father O'Malley leading the way and with six sturdy red-faced lads bearing the coffin the procession was moving towards me and my little gate. I stood aside to let them through. I tried to catch Father O'Malley's eye, but his head was deep in prayer and he was intoning aloud from a Missal as he led the mourners through the tiny opening and along the side of the church. He was heading for the graveyard beyond. I joined the procession, being swept along by a tide of mourners and all the time stretching my neck for sight of the foraging undertaker. I saw him dodging about, ducking behind tombstones as the multi-person crocodile crept around this sacred ground.

Luckily, he spotted me and ran towards me, tugging at my sleeve.

"I've been right round the place, there's no grave!" he hissed.

"How long's it take to dig one?" I asked him, thinking we might get Dusty to dig a large enough hole.

"All day," he said. My heart sank.

"I'll get Dusty," I said. "He's in the pub — maybe he's got the day wrong, or the time."

"What'll I do?"

"Keep 'em going round the churchyard until I get back," I said. "Father O'Malley's got his head down, so if you go in front and lead him round in circles he'll never notice. He'll just follow your heels."

"Those lads will drop the bloody coffin!" he cried. "It's heavy, you know, good solid oak. And Jim was a big bloke."

"They're tough youngsters," was all I could say as I hurried away.

I dashed from the churchyard and held onto my helmet as I ran down to the pub. George was just locking up and seemed surprised at my perspiring and panting figure.

"Thirsty, Mr Rhea?" he smiled. "I've just closed."

"Is Dusty here?" I panted.

"Nay, he went over to the church," he said. "Said summat about filling in Bathurst's grave."

"There is no grave!" I called. "He's forgotten to dig it."

"Forgotten?" cried George. "Not Dusty, he never forgets. It'll be there . . ."

So I left. I was running back when I recollected my earlier sighting of Dusty with his spade. If he had been going to the pub, which he was when I saw him, he hadn't come from the Catholic Church of St Francis of Assisi. A horrible thought dawned on me. I halted my gallop, turned on my heels and ran into the grounds of the Anglican parish church of St Andrew.

The place was full of tall tombstones and crosses, but in seconds I located him. He was standing against the wall at the far end of the churchyard. He saw me and waved his spade to draw my attention.

"Over here, Mr Rhea," he shouted.

"Dusty!" I was breathless as I came to rest before him. "Is this for James Bathurst?"

"Aye, it is," he confirmed.

"But it's in the wrong churchyard!" I panted. "It should have been over there, at St Francis."

"Nay, lad, it shouldn't," he clenched his teeth, placed the spade against the wall and crossed his arms. "This is t' right spot."

"No," I said, gaining my breath. "He became a Catholic on his deathbed, and his funeral is over there. Father O'Malley's looking for his grave right now."

"Then tell him it's here," said Dusty.

"But it's the wrong place, wrong religion . . ." I tried to explain.

"Nay, Mr Rhea. This is Bathurst territory, this piece of land. All his ancestors are here, every single one of 'em. This is where yon Mr Bathurst gets buried, not over there among all them papists."

"But he became a Papist . . . er Catholic," I tried. "It was his personal choice."

"On his deathbed, not in his right senses at the time. Nay, Mr Rhea, I can't accept that. Here he's buried or not at all," and his jaw jutted in an act of personal defiance.

I dithered for what seemed an eternity, then dashed back to the other church. The procession had done one complete circuit of the churchyard to the music of Father O'Malley's intonations — up one side, across the bank and down the other with everyone seeking the elusive hole in the ground. They were now setting off upon their second exploration and the lads bearing the coffin looked all in. Sweat was pouring from them and they would soon have to have a rest . . .

"Father." I hurried to the front of the queue and spoke quietly to him.

For a moment, he ignored me and I thought I'd get an Irish blasting, but he recognised the concern in my voice.

"Yes, my son?"

"The grave," I whispered. "It's over in the Anglican churchyard, with the Bathurst ancestors."

"Holy Mother of God!" he burst. "That bloody man Miller!"

"The lads with the coffin are nearly all in," I warned him. "What shall I do?"

"Keep walking beside me, my son, while I ponder this one," he said in his thick Irish brogue. "Now, what would God do in a situation like this? God would never get Himself into a situation like this, would He now? There's a hole in the ground over there and all holes in the ground are the same. Earth to earth, dust to dust. But it's not Catholic consecrated ground. It's Protestant land, fit only for sheep and hens. But he's a man, and a man needs a decent burial . . . most of us like to be with our loved ones in our eternal rest . . . but the Anglicans will be claiming him as theirs . . . but we get the proceeds of the will, eh? We sell the house for Catholic charities . . . we can use money to put a plaque in our church, so we can, telling the world where he's buried and how he was converted . . ."

I listened to his one-sided conversation and turned to look at the poor bearers. They were buckling at the knees, their eyes were bulging and their faces were red with the pain of their burden. Strong fit farm lads they were, but there is a limit . . .

"Rest awhile on the stone bench beneath the Anglican lych-gate," he said to them. "'Tis apparent he's to be buried at the other side."

Most adroitly, he guided the long, straggly procession around the graveyard and out onto the road. The grateful bearers placed the coffin on the slab beneath the lych-gate and the entire procession halted. Father O'Malley addressed them.

"It seems there's been a bit of poaching," he said. "Dusty's dug the grave at the wrong side of the road, so he has. So we'll bury him there, poor man. May the Lord have mercy on his soul."

And so, after a brief consultation with the vicar, James Bathurst was laid to rest among his ancestors and relations. I knew that Father O'Malley would erect a memorial plaque on the wall of St Francis of Assisi, so the truth would prevail. As we adjourned to the house for the traditional ham tea, Dusty lovingly filled in the grave and arranged the floral tributes about the new earth. He came into the house an hour later, ready for his refreshments and I saw one or two of the villagers congratulate him. I wondered if this had been Dusty's own idea, or whether some of the stalwarts had put him up to it.

But it didn't matter. With the coming world of ecumenical understanding was one grave any worse than any other?

The last word went to Father O'Malley. I was fortunate to be nearby as he cornered Dusty Miller over his cup of tea.

"Dusty Miller," he breathed at the little fellow. "This was all your doing, I'll be bound."

"He's resting in his rightful place," stated Dusty.

"Then you'll rest in my churchyard, Dusty Miller," said Father O'Malley. "If I can convert a Bathurst, I'll make short work of you, my lad. Mark my words, and like it or not, you will be buried in the churchyard of St Francis of Assisi. I'll get you, so help me!"

Dusty fled and I saw the glint of amusement in Father O'Malley's eye.

No worse fate could befall poor Dusty, for he was a very protesting Protestant.

* * *

That little incident served to bring together the two faiths, Anglican and Catholic, in Elsinby. The Rev. Simon Hamilton and Father Brendan O'Malley became even more friendly towards each other, although it must be said they had never shown any real antagonism. They served together on committees, lunched together regularly to discuss mutual problems and ambitions, and loaned each other various items of religious significance. All this had evolved long before the Bathurst funeral, but it was that burial with its last-minute compromise which sealed the friendship. One immediate result was that the Catholics traipsed into the Anglican churchyard on a regular, organised basis to pay open tribute to their celebrated convert, James Bathurst. Some had misgivings over this, but Father O'Malley dealt with their worries by buying the grave from the Anglicans. He paid a nominal sum, but it thus became Catholic ground. James Bathurst was now buried in a patch of Catholic ground, an island of saintly refuge in the middle of an Anglican graveyard. But at least he was among his Protestant forebears and friends, an ideal situation.

While Catholics could be seen pottering up and down those paths of Anglican ground, the Anglicans had no reason to do likewise so far as the Catholic church was concerned. Their reticence continued; the only occasion they entered the walls of St Francis of Assisi was for a local wedding or funeral, or when the two ministers of religion held a joint service, such as an ecumenical gathering or on Remembrance Day. Officially, a state of bliss existed but in practice the two faiths were poles apart.

A real test occurred late one summer. My first intimation was a telephone call from the Reverend Hamilton asking if I would pop in to see him next time I was on duty in Elsinby. I agreed and within a week I was in his study, enjoying a pleasant coffee.

He was a fine man, the Reverend Hamilton. With a faint Scots accent, he stood an impressive six feet tall and boasted an athletic past, having once played football for a Scottish First Division team. He was married to a lovely wife who happily joined the multifarious affairs of village life. The vicar considered himself very much part of the North Riding population even though he had been here a mere eight years. He reckoned he had adopted the county as his home.

But there was one grey cloud on his horizon. In spite of his popularity and his earnest efforts, the congregation of St Andrew's Parish Church continued to dwindle. Young folk didn't bother to attend, the middle-aged were too busy and the elderly too tired. Mr Hamilton relied on a regular attendance of some twenty faithful, swollen to fifty at times like Easter and Christmas, but this was in no way a proportional representation of the population. With over 350 people in the parish, his church looked miserably empty at most times.

Father O'Malley, on the other hand, had a Catholic congregation of some 180 souls, young, old and middle-aged, and he ensured they attended Mass every Sunday. They also came to other services as and when required. He averaged a hundred and ten each Sunday for Mass and this made the poor Anglican church look very poorly attended.

The unhappy Simon Hamilton told me all about this aspect of his work and he wondered how the Catholics managed to fill their church with youngsters when he failed; I told him I was a Catholic and attended Mass regularly at Aidensfield, and he raised his eyes to Heaven.

"You know, Mr Rhea," he said, with that faint Scots accent lingering in the air. "I could do with your faithful in a fortnight's time."

"Really?" I didn't quite understand his comment.

"Yes, I've called you here to discuss a small matter." I thought he'd gone off at a tangent, but he continued. "My bishop is coming a fortnight on Sunday. It's his first visit since his appointment three years ago, and that's why I called you in. I want to ensure everything goes well, and I need your advice on car-parking and traffic arrangements."

"I'll help, of course," I assured him, for supervision of such events was part of my duty.

"There's no car park at the church, as you know, so I'm afraid the bishop's car will have to park on the road outside."

"That's no problem," I said. "The road is wide enough to allow that."

"Yes, I'm sure it is. And there's the congregation's cars, plus the other clergy who come from neighbouring parishes. There might be a lot of cars, Mr Rhea, and I wondered if I could prevail upon you to ensure the bishop is parked as near as possible to the gate."

"I'll get here half an hour before the service," I assured him, "and I will make sure things go according to your wishes."

We discussed the outline plans for the day and I learned he was to prepare a feast in the parish rooms, at which the bishop would attend for the purpose of informally meeting the parishioners. Clearly, Mr Hamilton had a lot of work ahead, and I could see that he wanted the day to be a huge success.

Having explained everything to me, with details of timings and anticipated numbers, I could see he still looked rather apprehensive.

"You're not very happy about this?" I put to him.

He shook his head. "No," he sighed. "No, Mr Rhea, I'm not. It's the apathy."

"Apathy?"

"Yes, people don't come to church anymore and I've tried to talk those who never come into attending on that day. This church was once a flourishing community, full every Sunday with lots of activities, but now, well, I get my regulars — only a dozen or so — but no more."

"Surely they'll all come to meet the bishop?" I said.

"Ah, yes, they'll come, the regulars. But no one else. Well, I'm lying there — one or two extra people have expressed a desire to come, but I'll have more clergy there than lay congregation if I'm not careful. I would have liked a full church that day . . ."

"Is it just a social visit?" I asked, wondering whether this came under the heading of ecumenism, or whether it was a confirmation visit.

"Not really. It's an official inspection really, disguised as a social 'meet the people' outing. Bishops go around checking on us, very discreetly, to make sure we do our job. My God, Mr Rhea, I've worked, but I never seem to make headway . . ."

"If it was an ecumenical service, Father O'Malley's lot would come," I smiled. "They would fill your empty seats."

He rubbed his chin and smiled at me. "If I didn't know better, I'd swear you were trying to convince me that Catholicism was the answer to everything."

"It's not the answer to everything, Mr Hamilton, but it might be the answer to your immediate problem."

"You're not serious?" he cried, staring at me over his coffee-cup.

"Why not?" I returned. "Why not fill your church with Catholics?"

"The bishop would object . . . he'd know . . ."

"Not if you didn't tell him, not if Father O'Malley provided them with . . . er . . . how shall I put it . . . their terms of reference."

"But suppose the bishop talked to a Catholic who let the cat out of the bag and said he was from St Francis' across the road . . ."

"Then you talk to the bishop about the spirit of ecumenism. You tell him how the faiths mingle in the village and quote the Catholic presence as an example of the interest in his work by the Catholic community . . ."

"My church will seat nearly three hundred," he mused. "With a handful of locals and a few clergy hangers-on, it will look deserted. How many Catholics could he muster?"

"A churchful," I smiled. "If you issue that as a challenge to Father O'Malley, he'll fill your church with religious folk who will listen to your bishop and eat your sandwiches like good Anglicans."

He smiled, "You know, Mr Rhea, I find this very tempting. I would not wish to lie to the bishop, but a churchful of worshippers would look fine, and it would be impressive."

"Shall I intercede with Father O'Malley?" I suggested.

"No," he said. "No, I think this had better come from me. Look, I'll talk to him and let you know what transpires. Can I be in touch again about the car-parking?"

"Of course," and I left him.

Hardly had I got outside when I saw Sergeant Blaketon sitting in his official car with the window down. He was looking up and down the High Street and when he saw me emerge from the vicarage he left the car. He strode stiffly towards me.

"Good afternoon, Rhea," he greeted me. "I saw your bike. Busy?"

"I've been to a meeting with the vicar," I told him. "He's got an official visit by his bishop shortly, and wanted me to help with car parking."

"Do you anticipate problems?" he asked. "We can fix you up with parking cones or another constable if you wish."

"No, I'll manage," I said and added thoughtlessly, "I don't anticipate a lot of cars."

"Oh, does that mean a poor congregation?" he asked me. "Even for a bishop's visit?"

"He's working on ideas for filling the church," I said. "He's a man of great imagination, is our vicar."

"What he needs is a few Methodists to help out," I heard him say. "Now, I'm a keen chapel-goer, and in these days of ecumenism it's good for the faiths to mingle."

I began to wish I'd accepted his cones and additional policeman.

"I'm sure he will fill the church." I tried to steer him away from his topic, but he was not to be swayed.

"Not with Catholics?" he looked at the modern outline of the St Francis of Assisi Church just behind.

"I think there are enough Anglicans hereabouts to provide him with a full house," I said.

"Not on your life," he retorted. "I'll speak to our local minister at the chapel. We might come along to support him. When did you say it was?"

I provided him with the date and groaned inwardly. I hoped he'd stay out of this. We went for a long walk around Elsinby, with Sergeant Blaketon expounding the merits of inter-religious exchanges and the need for more discipline among the young. I wondered if the two were connected, but he lost me in a sea of hazy words as I worried about the possible outcome of his idea. I tried to deter him but he was not to be deflected.

A week later, I was back in Elsinby and decided to call upon Father O'Malley. I found him making wine in his kitchen and he invited me to sample a glassful of last year's vintage. It was beetroot wine, a beautiful red colour, and it tasted like fine port.

"Your health, Nicholas." He raised his own glass. "What brings you here?"

"I was passing," I said, "and thought I'd pop in."

"You did right, so you did," he smiled through his strong teeth. He looked a typical Irishman, with bushy black hair and firm eyebrows set in a strong face, full of character. "How's the wine?"

"Fine." I sipped appreciatively. "Father, has Mr Hamilton seen you about a service at the parish church?"

"He has, yes he has. And a nice idea too."

He paused and sipped the wine, then added, "He tells me it was your idea."

"Well, I thought we might do a little for ecumenism."

"And so we will. I've already mentioned it to some of the faithful here and we'll fill the church for him, to be sure. It's a challenge to these people, Nicholas, and it's a way for them to get their own back for Jimmy Bathurst's funeral. But I've asked them all to behave like good Anglicans that day."

"I hope it doesn't backfire on him."

"No, it won't. I'll see to that. I'll be there too."

"In your collar?"

"No, I will dress as an Irish labourer that day, so help me. Never you worry, Nicholas. We'll give his bishop a day to remember. We've already agreed on the hymns that will be sung, and my lot are in full training. They'll sing some lovely Anglican hymns, mark my words."

So far as the arrangements for the service were concerned, I knew I had no worries. The two clergymen had come to a fine, sensible agreement and my next involvement was on the actual day of the bishop's visit.

The service was to begin at 3 p.m. that Sunday and it would last for an hour, with twenty minutes being allowed for an address by the bishop. Tea had been arranged in the parish rooms during which the bishop would mingle with the faithful on an informal basis. Those Catholics who felt they might behave erratically need not attend, for the tiny room could not accommodate everyone.

On the big day, I took my motorcycle into the grounds of the Hopbind Inn and left it there with George's permission, replacing my helmet with a uniform cap. At two-thirty, I took up my position outside the St Andrew's church gate to keep a space free for the visiting dignitary. Cars began to arrive about twenty minutes to three and all greeted me warmly. Mr Hamilton came out to check that all was well, and the sun shone upon his little castle. I bade "good afternoon" to many good Anglicans and lots of equally good Catholics, all filing into the sombre walls of the church to be issued with hymn-books upon entry. Father O'Malley was there too, dressed in rough clothes but beaming all over his rugged face.

"'Tis good to understand the ways of the Lord, Nicholas," he smiled as he strode towards the imposing entrance.

I looked at my watch. Ten minutes to three. The bishop was due in five minutes.

Mr Hamilton came along the path ready to meet him and we stood together, looking anxiously along the High Street.

"Will he be on time?" I asked.

"I'm sure he will, he's been to a morning service south of York, and he lunched in the city with the archbishop. He'll be on time."

"The last bishop never visited Elsinby?" I put to him as we waited.

"No," he said. "All those occasions when a bishop was needed, like confirmations, were held in Aidensfield, so we never got a visit. But this chap's changed all that, he's visiting every church in his diocese."

At five minutes to three I heard an approaching vehicle.

A large, luxury coach materialised around the corner and I was horrified to see Sergeant Blaketon's huge figure standing near the front door. The bus halted right before us with a squeal of brakes and Sergeant Blaketon, in full uniform, clambered down. It had parked right in the bishop's place.

"Afternoon, Vicar, afternoon, Rhea," he beamed at us.

"Mr Hamilton, this is Sergeant Blaketon from Ashfordly, my section station. Sergeant, the Reverend Simon Hamilton, the vicar of Elsinby."

They shook hands, and Blaketon said, "I heard you needed a congregation, Vicar, so I've got a bus-load of Methodists with me, all from Ashfordly."

"A congregation, Sergeant?"

"Yes, young Rhea let it drop that you couldn't fill the church, so I thought it would be a nice gesture of working Christianity if I brought along a few of my friends, just to fill the gaps, in a manner of speaking."

"Er, it's very kind of you, Sergeant, but I think you'll find my church is full. But go in, please — it might be standing room only."

"Come along, you lot," bawled Sergeant Blaketon in a good-humoured way. "Fill up that church like good Anglicans."

And as they descended from their coach I saw the oncoming procession with its Austin Princess at the lead. The bishop was here.

"Sarge!" I cried. "That bus is on the bishop's parking-place."

"We won't be a minute, lad."

"But he's here, coming up the village now!"

There was a moment of confusion, as Sergeant Blaketon tried to get the driver to move before everyone was out, but he failed. The slow-moving stream of Methodists held up the coach and the result was that the bishop's car had to park a few yards away. I was upset but the bishop didn't seem to mind.

He and his attendants dismounted and I saw he was a little, jovial man with a round happy face and dancing eyes.

"Full house, eh?" he beamed, looking at the coach. "Am I early?"

"No, Your Grace," smiled Mr Hamilton. "When they get inside, I will take you in."

"Let us not hurry those good people," the bishop said, looking at me. "And this is your local policeman?"

"P.C. Rhea, from Ashfordly, Your Grace." I extended my hand and he shook it warmly with a firm grip.

"It's nice of you to help us out," smiled the bishop as he watched the last of Blaketon's faithful enter the church. The bus moved away and the bishop's chauffeur slid into his correct position. Everything was just as it should be.

"Are you going in?" asked the bishop of me.

"I am, Your Grace," and I went ahead, leaving the bishop and the vicar to enter last. As I edged my way into the packed church, I could see people everywhere. The place was packed and Sergeant Blaketon's Methodists were standing in the aisles down the side and at the rear. It was a wonderful sight.

Sergeant Blaketon saw me enter and I was compelled to stand close to him. "Rhea," he whispered hoarsely, "This place is full of bloody papists."

"Is it, Sergeant?" I smiled as the organ struck up with the first hymn.

As the bishop walked down the aisle, the Anglicans, Catholics and Methodists burst into a rousing hymn of welcome, each faith trying to outsing the other. The harmonious Methodists sang with their usual blend of religious fervour and elegance and perhaps theirs was the better music. But it was a joyful welcome and everyone settled down for the start of this memorable service.

It was a splendid occasion by any standards. The singing was good enough to lift the ancient roof of this church, and everyone joined in with the utmost enthusiasm. The Catholics almost forgot to add the tailpiece at the end of the "Our Father", but Father O'Malley's stentorian tones led them into that final act of homage. By four o'clock it was all over, and the congregation reckoned the bishop's address had been first rate. He had talked wholeheartedly of harmony between Christians and I wondered if he knew how apt his words were on this occasion.

During the tea afterwards, everyone mingled and ate happily, and I was pleased to see local Catholics chatting with local Methodists interspaced with Anglicans. The bishop in his purple mingled too and I saw him chatting earnestly with several of the Catholics of St Francis. But it all went very, very well indeed. Mr Hamilton beamed benevolently upon everyone.

His Grace was scheduled to leave at five fifteen and I positioned myself near his car to ensure a smooth departure. He was five or ten minutes late leaving and I saluted him as he came through the door. There he paused a moment, and said, "You know, Officer, the Pope would have been proud of that turn-out, eh?"

"Yes, Your Grace," I smiled as he departed. As the car swept along the village High Street, I turned to find Sergeant Blaketon standing at my elbow.

"I don't suppose you had anything to do with this, Rhea?" he growled.

"With what, Sergeant?"

"Packing that church with papists?"

"If I was an insurance agent, Sergeant, I would record it as an Act of God," I said, turning back to find another cup of tea.

\* \* \*

I never really knew whether Sergeant Blaketon disliked members of the Roman Catholic Church, or whether his remarks were deep-seated jokes understood only by himself. In truth, there were few occasions when religion entered my work as a village policeman, but I must confess that on one occasion the rigid faith of a little old lady completely thwarted me.

To put the story in perspective, it began with the death of a Mr Abraham Potter whose home was a lovely cottage in Aidensfield, just up the street from the pub. Awd Abe, as everyone affectionately called him, had been a lifelong Methodist of the strictest kind, never drinking liquor, never smoking, never swearing, never gambling and never working on Sundays. He led an exemplary life and was a true pillar of the chapel. There, he cleaned and gardened, painted and decorated and wrote the notices for Sunday in his beautiful copper-plate handwriting. Then he died.

My arrival at Aidensfield coincided with his death, so I never met Awd Abe. From his reputation, I guessed his name would live on as an example of righteousness and Christian standards. His death meant that his little cottage would be sold and, within a few weeks, the "For Sale" signs appeared in the garden. His relatives had been traced and had agreed to sell the house, but no one had foreseen the conditions he'd imposed upon the sale.

I learned of these by pure chance, for I was patrolling the village street as the estate agents were erecting their "For Sale" boards. As village constables are wont to do, I stopped for a chat.

"Will it sell?" I asked, for rural properties at that time were not fetching very high prices. It was before the boom in country cottages.

"It would, if it wasn't for Awd Abe," said the man.

"He's dead," I remarked, wondering if he knew.

"Aye, we know, but he's left a will saying what's got to be done with this spot, if his nephews sell it."

"Has he? What's he said?" I was interested now.

"You knew him?" the man put to me.

I shook my head. "No, he died just before I was posted here."

"Big chapel man, he was," I was told. "Very straight sort of a chap. Lived by the Bible, you know."

"So I've heard." Awd Abe's reputation lived on.

"Well, he's put conditions on the sale of this spot," the man told me guardedly. "I reckon we'll have a job selling it."

"What sort of conditions?"

"Well," he said. "First, it mustn't be sold to or occupied by a Roman Catholic. And the person that buys it must not read Sunday papers, mustn't play cards, mustn't drink alcohol, mustn't have children, mustn't keep animals, mustn't smoke, mustn't gamble and mustn't work on Sundays. And they must be regular attenders at chapel, not church."

"He *will* have a job selling it here!" I laughed. "Practically every other family is Catholic and I imagine most folks nowadays read Sunday papers . . . why the Sunday papers bit?"

"He didn't believe in working on the Sabbath," said the estate agent's man. "Anything that had been created on the Sabbath must not enter his house. He didn't even wash up on Sundays, he was that pernickety about his faith."

"But the papers are printed on Saturdays," I said.

"Aye, lots of folk told him that, and they told him about factories making furniture on Sunday, or canning food, farmers working, doctors and so on . . ."

"But he wouldn't give?"

"Not him," said the man. "And when we got this house to sell, well, we all laughed. I mean, who's going to buy it? Who can truthfully agree to those conditions?"

"Search me!" I smiled and went on my way. Lots of the locals would have loved his cottage for it was pleasantly located and well-built, but Awd Abe's conditions immediately placed it beyond the reach of local folks.

But it did sell.

Word must have spread far afield because a little old lady called Miss Sarah Prudom arrived to inspect the cottage. I didn't see her arrival, but learned she came from the Doncaster area and was seeking a place in the country for retirement. She'd worked as a laundry manageress, I was told.

As things turned out, Miss Prudom perfectly fitted Awd Abe's specification. Furthermore, she was an unmarried lady of spotless virtue, and we all felt Abe would have been proud of her. I wondered if they might have married, had they met in life, but perhaps such associations could lead to sins of the flesh. Anyway, Miss Prudom bought Awd Abe's cottage.

One fine spring day, she moved in with her furniture and books and there is little doubt that her arrival in

Aidensfield brought hope to the tiny chapel flock. Abe had gone but his place had been taken by an equally enthusiastic worker, as indeed she was. Miss Prudom soon busied herself about the chapel and fussed over the congregation, visiting them, talking to them, praising them and arranging prayer meetings from time to time.

As the weeks rolled by, it was quite evident that she fitted perfectly Awd Abe's specifications. She was a lovely little woman, both in charm and in appearance. Her trim figure graced the village as she went about her daily business, for she was always smartly dressed and wore rimless spectacles which seemed to shine beneath her grey hair. Rose-coloured cheeks and a ready smile completed her charming appearance and everyone liked her.

Then, one day, she appeared to break her strict rules, because she appeared in the village store one Sunday morning. The store opened from 10.30 a.m. until twelve noon, and was patronised by the Catholics as they left Mass, and by others who forgot bits and pieces on Saturdays. The uncharacteristic appearance of Miss Prudom in the shop caused something of a stir, and I was in at the time, just passing the time of day.

She blushed as she entered, for she must have known that all present knew of her strict beliefs, but the shopkeeper calmly asked, "Yes, Miss Prudom?"

"I have friends calling for tea," she said confidentially, "and they have just telephoned to inform me. I have nothing in the house. Could I have a tin of smoked salmon please, and a lettuce and some tomatoes?"

"Certainly."

She wanted other items too, and ticked them off a handwritten list as the shopkeeper busied himself with her order. Finally, her basket was full.

"How much is that?" she asked smiling.

"One pound, five shillings and threepence," he said.

"Will you take a cheque?" she asked him.

"Of course, I will be pleased."

She opened her cheque-book on the counter and wrote in the correct amount, then said, "I have dated it for tomorrow, will that be all right?"

"Yes, of course, Miss Prudom."

After handing over the cheque, she smiled graciously at him and said, "Thank you, Mr Woodall, it is most kind of you to allow me to do that. You see, I cannot buy goods on the Sabbath, so this means I've bought, them tomorrow, Monday. You have got me out of a dilemma, and I appreciate it deeply."

"I'm always pleased to help," and she was gone.

I was amazed at her logic, but have since come across similar faithful who bend the rules, such as those who refuse to drink alcohol, but who buy in bottles of brandy or whisky for medicinal purposes.

But it was Miss Prudom and her religious beliefs which caused me a headache.

Several months later, her house was burgled. I do not think she was wealthy, but her prim little home did contain some pleasing items of crockery and glassware, in addition to several good pieces of silver plate. These were family heirlooms. Sometime between nine o'clock one Saturday night and six o'clock the next morning, Sunday, a villain broke into her home and stole silver and crockery worth about £200. He entered through the rear kitchen window, which he broke in order to release the catch, climbed in and ransacked the downstairs rooms while she was asleep.

As Miss Prudom rose early on the Sabbath, she discovered the horror just after six and the shock was so great that she did nothing until nine o'clock. As I learned afterwards, she'd simply sat and wept at the sight of her personal belongings strewn across the floor, and at the thought of a strange, uncouth man rifling her treasures as she slept. At nine o'clock, she rang Ashfordly Police Station to report the crime.

Alwyn Foxton was on duty and chanced to be in the office. He listened sympathetically and asked her not to touch anything. He told her he would despatch a policeman immediately to the scene. Alwyn then telephoned me, for I was on duty that Sunday.

"I'll go straight there," I said.

Within minutes, I had donned my crash-helmet and heavy coat against the threat of April showers and within two minutes of leaving my hilltop house I was drawing up beside Miss Prudom's cottage. She came to the door to greet me and her ashen face and red-rimmed eyes told of her solitary distress.

"I'm P.C. Rhea," I announced. "Your local policeman — we haven't met formally."

"You were in the shop the other morning," she said seriously.

"Yes, I often pop in to talk with Mr Woodall."

"It's awful, Mr Rhea, the mess. Just to think that somebody has been in there, while I was in bed, going through my belongings . . ."

"I'll examine the house first, to give a quick assessment, and then I'll call the C.I.D. They'll come to fingerprint the house and examine it for other clues . . ."

"Oh, you can't come in," she said pertly. "I'm sorry."

"But I need to, Miss Prudom. It's vital that the police come in to examine the scene of the crime. We can't make a proper investigation without seeing for ourselves . . ."

"No, you don't understand. Mr Rhea, you are a Catholic, aren't you?"

"Yes, I am," I confirmed.

"But you see, I do not allow papists into my home. I never have and never will. And today is Sunday too. You must know of Mr Potter's conditions of sale, about Catholics not entering or buying this house . . ."

"But, Miss Prudom, it is my job. If I am to have even the remotest chance of detecting this crime, I must come inside to see how the criminal has gone about his work. And I need to talk to you, to take a statement from you, to ask about identification of the stolen goods and a host of other things, like values and detailed descriptions . . ."

"I'm sorry, Mr Rhea," was all she said.

I stood on the doorstep looking at her. She was a sad picture; her eyes were rimmed with red and her pretty face was pale and drawn. She was wringing her hands before her frail body as she kept me at bay and I must admit I didn't know how to tackle this problem. I felt desperately sorry for her.

"Can I see the window then, at the back? I can examine it from the outside. That will be a help."

"Yes, that will be all right."

She led me to the rear of the house and I examined the smashed window-pane. It had been broken with some heavy object, and pieces of glass lay inside, on the window-ledge. Chummy had opened the latch, climbed in and ransacked the place, leaving by the front door with his loot.

I made notes of this, which was all I could see.

Back at the front door, I smiled at her. I remembered one little item.

"Miss Prudom," I said. "You were in the shop the other Sunday and you bought some food."

"Yes."

"That was an emergency, wasn't it? And I noticed how you paid by cheque, dated Monday, to avoid buying them on the Sabbath."

"Yes, but it was a dire emergency . . ."

"Then so is this. The police might be able to catch the criminal if we can come inside . . . I could always date my reports tomorrow, you see . . ."

"You miss the point, Mr Rhea. The point is that papists must not enter my house. That is the point, it's nothing to do with the Sabbath."

"If Christ lived here, would He let me enter?" I asked her.

She remained very silent and her bright eyes regarded me solemnly, before adding, "But He doesn't live here. I do."

I felt like quoting the Parable of the Lost Sheep but knew I was fighting a losing battle. "Well, Miss Prudom, what can I do? A crime has been committed on my beat, and

I am responsible for recording the fact and investigating the matter. I cannot do my work, which could lead to the arrest of the criminal, without examining your house."

"Mr Rhea," she smiled sweetly. "I have nothing against you personally. You must realise that. It has long been the practice in my family never to associate with or to encourage popery in any shape or form. You must allow me to exercise my principles."

"Even if it means post-dating a cheque to allow you to buy goods on the Sabbath?" I was angry now and utterly failed to understand the hypocrisy in her. I could have argued all day and all night but it would not have made any difference to her bigotry. I knew it would be unchristian of me to begin a pitched theological battle on her doorstep, and besides, she had suffered the ignominy of a burglary. I did not wish to add to her obvious distress.

I left, saying, "I'll get another officer to call on you."

It was with some sadness, therefore, that I returned to my house on the hill and telephoned the office at Ashfordly. As Alwyn Foxton answered the telephone, my experience of the bishop's visit to Elsinby came to mind.

"Is Sergeant Blaketon there?" I asked.

"I'll put you through," he said.

"Blaketon," came the solemn response. "Something wrong, Rhea?"

"I've a problem I think you might solve for me, Sergeant."

"Oh, something you can't cope with?" I thought I detected a faint hint of sarcasm in his voice.

"Yes," I said, "a woman."

"Women are always problematical," he propounded. "I thought a young lad like you would be able to charm a woman."

"Not this one," I said. "She's a fierce chapel-going Methodist."

"So?" he boomed.

"So she won't let me into her house to investigate a burglary," I said, "and if any of the C.I.D. are Catholics they won't be allowed in either."

He roared with laughter. I could hear him at the other end of the line, chortling in his happiness as I explained the problem.

"Nice one, Rhea, yes, a very nice one. Serve you right for getting our Anglican church full of papists the other week. Right, leave it to me. I'm with Miss Prudom on this one. I'll sort it out."

And so he did. She allowed him to enter her premises whereupon she provided all the necessary help and information. The C.I.D. were called too and Sergeant Blaketon first warned them not to bring a Catholic — she'd know if they did, he warned them. She could smell 'em. Through his help, the crime was reported in the formal way and the necessary documents were completed. Miss Prudom provided a very detailed list of all the stolen goods and in the course of the next few days we circulated the information to all police offices in the locality. This was standard procedure.

Sadly, the burglar was never found. He committed several similar crimes in and around the North Riding over the next few months, and then he stopped. His hallmark was the method of entry and exit, and the type of property he took, but we never caught him. Perhaps another police force came across him, perhaps he was arrested elsewhere. We shall never know.

The sequel to the yarn, however, was the criminal's return of a photograph. It showed a very young Miss Prudom with her father and it was endorsed to that effect on the rear. The picture was probably fifty years old or more and I'm sure it was of sentimental value to her. For that reason, it was returned to her through the post.

She called at my police house to inform me of this event and I invited her in so that I could amend the list of stolen goods. She entered my house without hesitation and we concluded that piece of official business. I considered questioning her ethics on this occasion, but decided against it.

She'd probably say the police house didn't qualify in her rule-book due to its official function, so I didn't ask. There seemed to be no point.

# CHAPTER SIX

What is this that roareth thus?
Can it be a motor bus?
ALFRED DENIS GODLER, 1856—1925

One of the inescapable features of a police officer's life is to be told incessantly about parking tickets. In company, the moment one's true occupation is known, out come all the harrowing tales of parking problems; he is told how the speaker parked only for the briefest of moments while he changed his library book/bought himself underpants/ waited for the wife/suffered from dampness on his coil or got involved in some other accident of history. Never is a motorist at fault in such circumstances; everyone else is, especially the police.

Police officers who suffer from such ear-bending sessions can sympathise with doctors who are bored about operations, solicitors who are cornered by convicted innocents and plumbers who can't get away from rattling taps or overflowing cisterns. For this reason, policemen who go on holiday seldom admit their true occupation — only a masochist would do that. Holidaying constables announce to their audience that they are variously employed as clerks for the government, officers in local authority employment, out-of-work salesmen, bingo callers or members of other sundry occupations. I know one policeman who, when on holiday, always tells his new-found friends that he is a button sales-man. He reckons that's the best conversation-stopper there is — after all, what can anyone ask about that?

One of my constabulary pals was on holiday in Scotland when this problem arose. Paul was with his wife and they had booked into a beautiful bed-and-breakfast farmhouse in the Highlands intending to stay overnight. So nice was the place that they stayed the entire week, and found the only other residents were another gentleman and his wife. They became friendly, especially over the evening meal and at breakfast. As the week progressed, Paul realised that the other gentleman never once gave a clue to his own occupation. Moreover, he never asked Paul how he earned his living.

The state of unspoken bliss continued through the week and on the final breakfast morning, that Saturday, Paul decided to tackle the other about his job. All through the week, he had realised the other was being overcautious about his work and decided to put him to the test.

At breakfast, therefore, he said, "Look, Jonathan, let's be honest, eh? You and I have been carefully avoiding any discussion about our jobs, haven't we? All this week, you have carefully avoided talking about your work and so have I."

The other smiled agreeably. "I don't like to talk about my job when I'm on holiday."

"Neither do I," smiled Paul in return. "But this is our last morning together. By lunchtime, we'll be on our way home. Let's tell each other."

The other smiled again. "All right," he nodded. "Who's first?"

"I raised the matter," Paul admitted. "So I'll start. I'm a policeman."

"And I'm a bishop," said his friend.

For the country constable, however, such anonymity cannot be enjoyed. If he walks into the shop, pub, church or meeting of any kind, he is always "the policeman" and his wife is always "the policeman's wife". When visiting one's local pub, therefore, it is impossible to be anything other than the local bobby, even when dressed in gardening clothes and covered in non-artificial farmyard waste products.

This being so, the talk often turns to motoring adventures in alien cities, of being stopped for speeding, booked for parking, checked for one's driving licence and insurance or pulled up for faulty windscreen-wipers. But at least in Aidensfield, I had a variation of this eternal theme.

I had a man who talked about buses.

It was soon very clear that he could talk about nothing else. For that reason, it became something of a trial to enter the pub knowing he lurked in the shadows, waiting to pounce on someone with his latest piece of juicy information about a 52-seater with reclining seats. I did my best to avoid him, as did every other regular in the bar of the Brewers Arms. They had had their fill of Plaxton Shells, Wallace Arnold tours and United Express runs with rural bus-stops.

At first, the fellow was interesting. I listened enthralled as he discussed the merits of demisters on side-windows and emergency exits near the front, tool-boxes under the offside exterior and double-deckers on rural routes, but when one has this indigestible manna during every visit it does begin to pall. I didn't know a great deal about buses anyway, but wondered how much this fellow really knew. Was it all conjecture and legend, or did he really know a lot about buses?

His name was Arnold Merryweather and he would be in his early fifties. He was a genial fellow, heavily built with a thick head of ginger hair and bushy side-whiskers, and he loved Irish jokes and Guinness. He was the life and soul of the pub, and his stories were funny, even if they were all about buses.

Arnold drove the bus which crept around our lanes day after day, week after week, to collect passengers at Ashfordly and transport them through the picturesque lanes and villages into York. His bus left Ashfordly at 7.30 a.m. and trundled through Briggsby, Aidensfield, Elsinby, and then beyond the boundaries of my beat and eventually into York. It did a return trip around lunchtime and turned about immediately for York. It arrived in time to turn round in the City at 5.15 p.m. to bring home the diminishing army of workers. Every day, week in week out, Arnold's bus undertook those journeys.

On Tuesdays, Thursdays and Saturdays, he left York immediately upon first arrival and did a special market-day run, collecting at Ashfordly at ten o'clock and getting into York around 11.30 a.m., having done a circuitous tour of Ryedale to get there. He was just able to fulfil his timetable with this extra trip and there's little doubt he earned his money on those important three days. Those earnings probably lasted him all week.

I learned eventually that Arnold owned the bus. He did not operate for any company, but earned his living entirely by his bus. During the evenings, he would arrange tours to cinemas in York, or to the theatre, and he did runs to the seaside and works outings to breweries and other places of interest. He did a school run too, collecting a rowdy horde of children from isolated places and risking his bus and its passengers on gradients of 1-in-3 as he visited outlying farms and hamlets. But Arnold always got there and very rarely was he late. His purple and cream bus, with "Merryweather Coaches" emblazoned across the rear, was a familiar sight in the hills and valleys of Aidensfield and district.

To fulfil his many commitments, he had two coaches, and had a standby driver employed to assist when necessary. But if it was possible to use one bus and one driver for his complicated timetables then Arnold did so.

I made use of his bus once or twice. Sometimes, if the weather was atrocious and if Mary was using the car, I would catch Arnold's bus at Aidensfield if I had business in Elsinby or Briggsby. I always paid, although he did offer me free transportation, for I reckoned he must be struggling to earn a living for himself and his colourless wife called Freda. He had to maintain his vehicles and premises too.

To partake of a trip on Merryweather Coaches was an experience which could be classed as unique. Each bus was identical and I think they were Albion 32-seaters. The seats were made of wooden laths set on iron frames and bolted to the floor. There were no cushions and other comforts, and the door was at the front. It was hinged in the middle and required a good kick from Arnold both to shut it and open it. Arnold acted as driver, conductor and guide as his precious heap of metal navigated the landscape.

My infrequent trips on his coaches proved to be an education. In the few flights I had, I saw him take on board one pig on a halter, three crates of chickens, a sheep and its lamb, a side of ham, several parcels and packages, a bicycle for repair, umpteen suits for cleaning or laundry for washing in York, and on one occasion he transported an unused coffin from Elsinby's undertaker to a man at Ashfordly who wanted it for timber.

These assorted objects were loaded into the bus via the rear emergency door and I learned that Arnold was paid for these sociable services. In addition to being a carrier of people, he was a carrier of objects and this was accepted quite amicably by his human cargo. If Farmer Jones wished to send a pig to Farmer Brown twenty miles away, Arnold would deliver the said animal by bus for a small fee. It seemed a perfectly sound system, but its legality was in grave doubt.

I knew Arnold had been in buses since leaving school and I reckoned he'd put himself on the road long before officials like the Traffic Commissioners appeared with their P.S.V. licences, certifying officers, certificates of fitness and road service licences. Nonetheless, he displayed in his windscreen the various discs which proved someone knew he was operating a bus service. Even so, the other rules and regulations seemed to be superfluous so far as Merryweather's Coaches were concerned.

His transportation of goods for hire or reward, for example, seemed to put him in the category of a goods vehicle rather than a bus, but it would be a stupid constable who attempted to stop that. After all, the fellow had to earn a living and he was doing a service to the community. I knew lots of house-bound folks depended upon Arnold for their weekly shopping, for he also spent his non-driving hours in York carrying out shopping requests for pensioners, invalids and others. He dealt with the parcels and packages on his bus, suits for the tailor to repair, carpets for the cleaners to clean, sewing-machines to mend, bikes to sell — the whole of society and its well-being made use of Arnold's bus.

Late one winter evening, I was pleased I tolerated his unofficial enterprises. My little Francis Barnet motorcycle broke down due to the driving rain which had penetrated the electrical circuits, and the faithful machine completely refused to go. The savagery of the storm meant I could find no place to dry the connections, then salvation arrived in the shape of Arnold's bus. He had taken a trip to the Theatre Royal in York to see a pantomime and his returning headlights picked me out in the appalling weather. Realising my predicament, Arnold hauled his laden coach to a halt and shouted:

"Stick it in t' back, Mr Rhea."

The rear door was flung open and several willing villagers leapt out. In a matter of seconds, they had manhandled my dripping motorcycle into the back and we rode home in triumph with the inactive bike held upright by pantomime visitors in their best clothes. Arnold refused to accept payment for this assistance, so I promised to buy him a pint in the pub. For me that would be a real penance because he'd bend my ear for an hour or two on the merits of diesel oil for buses or left-hand-drive models for continental tours.

Even I failed fully to appreciate Arnold's complete service to the public until I took his bus into York one market-day when I was off duty. Mary had a lot of shopping to do and Mrs Quarry took the children; the car was due for a service and it seemed a great idea to make use of Arnold's comprehensive bus service. Armed with baskets and money, therefore, we waited at Aidensfield one Tuesday morning for Arnold's market-day special. We were surrounded by little old ladies and retired gentlemen, all wondering why we had chosen this mode of transport, and we said it was because of Arnold's world-wide reputation as a busman.

Halfway between Aidensfield and Elsinby, Arnold halted and switched off the engine. We were parked in the middle of nowhere — no houses, no village, no bus-stop. Nothing. No one spoke. They all sat there very quietly and I watched Arnold in his driving-seat. He was reading the *Daily Mirror*. I checked my watch. We were running according to schedule. The fuel was all right, as he'd switched off the engine.

"Why have we stopped?" Mary ventured to ask in a whispered voice.

"I don't know," I had to admit. I didn't dare make a fool of myself by asking the others.

Nothing happened. We must have waited a good ten minutes and by this time we were running late.

Then, as one, the assortment of passengers sighed with relief. I looked out of the window to my nearside and noticed a distant figure hurrying along a winding farm track. It was a farmer's wife, laden with baskets.

I recognised her as she approached.

"It's Mrs Owens," I said to Mary.

"She always goes to market on Tuesdays," breathed Mary. "I've heard her talk about it in the shop. I didn't realise she lived down that lane."

I learned that Mrs Owens travelled on Arnold's bus every Tuesday and he always waited for her. Today she was a little late, but then that could happen to anyone. And so the bus continued.

The next diversion was about a mile out of Elsinby. Suddenly, we swung off the road and along a narrow tarmac lane. We trundled along this winding track for nearly half a mile and then Arnold turned his bus through a farm gate. We were now on a muddy track full of potholes and thick with half-buried rocks. Grass grew down the centre but Arnold's groaning, bouncing old bus negotiated this rough terrain and came to rest in a grubby farmyard.

At this point, he began to crash the gears, seeking reverse. Eventually, with a shudder, the gear slotted home and he began the difficult manoeuvre of turning the bus within the confines of the farmyard. Chickens and ducks scattered, dogs barked and a horse stared in amazement as the purple and cream vehicle moved slowly forwards and backwards, turning gradually until it was facing the way it had come.

"Now what?" Mary grinned.

"A load of manure?" I ventured.

The engine died and someone threw open the rear door. Out jumped about a dozen passengers, just as they had done for my motorcycle, and I watched them march towards a small outbuilding. The door was opened and they collected trays of packed eggs. Dozens and dozens of eggs. They bore these to the rear of the bus and began to stack them carefully, each tray bearing a dozen fresh farmyard eggs. Gradually the pile grew until it was as high as the shoulders of the seated people, and a second pile began. I lost count but I knew there was an awful lot of eggs. Without a word, all the volunteer loaders climbed aboard and closed the door.

But Arnold did not move yet. He waited until a tiny farm lady appeared. She wore a dull green mackintosh, black wooden clogs and a headscarf about her head. She carried a butter-basket in one hand and a hessian bag in the other, climbed aboard, asked for a "York return" and settled in a front seat.

And so it continued. We took children to catch trains, old folks to visit relatives in hospital, but the most amazing was Arnold's action in York City. The eggs were bound for York market which is tucked behind the city in a narrow marketplace. Because of sheer numbers, it was impossible to carry them from Arnold's terminus, so he took his bus and its load right into the marketplace and halted near a stall.

There, the reverse procedure was adopted; the rearmost passengers flung open the door and the clog-shod little woman masterminded the operation from outside. Every tray of eggs was delivered to the market trader who counted them and paid in cash, as Arnold sat in his seat, ignoring the hoots of protest from cars and vans around him. As the job was under way, he disgorged his other passengers and retreated to his official bus-stop, there to offload his grocery orders, parcels and messages.

After that first trip, it was a regular sight to see the familiar shape of Arnold's bus jolting along farm tracks, or turning around in stackyards, as it took aboard the produce of the district. Arnold's contribution to the economy of Ryedale was immense. Although he was supposed to follow a prescribed route, he totally ignored it and went wherever he was needed. Somehow he knew who was waiting on any particular day and he provided what amounted to a house-to-house bus service. Furthermore, it was expected of him.

With a service of this nature, coupled with his unauthorised diversion into the city centre, it was inevitable that the Traffic Commissioners would learn of his methods. I waited for that day with some trepidation. But it wasn't the Traffic Commissioners who caused my first legal brush with Arnold — it was Claude Jeremiah Greengrass.

\* \* \*

Arnold halted his creaking bus at my shoulder one morning as I walked through Aidensfield *en route* to the post office. His face was like thunder and he was in a highly agitated state. This was most unlike him — Arnold was usually the epitome of pleasantry and *bonhomie*, but it was clear that trouble was afoot.

"Mr Rhea," he hailed me by leaning out of his window.

"Morning, Arnold. Something wrong?"

"I'll say there is." He left his seat and emerged from the bus. On the street, he took my arm and steered me from the flapping ears of his passengers. "It's that bloody man Greengrass."

"Claude Jeremiah? What's he done to you?"

"He's pinching my customers, that's what."

"You don't mean to say he's bought a bus!" I cried, horrified at the ramifications of this and remembering the problems of the pigs and donkey.

"No, he's got an old car, a right old heap it is, Mr Rhea. He's running it ahead of me on my market-day runs, picking folks up and charging them less than me. He's ruining me."

"He can't get many in his car, surely?" I said, wondering what sort of enterprise Claude Jeremiah had evolved.

"I've seen him with seven packed into that old Austin," Arnold growled. "And he comes back before me, charging each customer sixpence less than me. He's taking trade off me, Mr Rhea. He'll have to be stopped."

"I'll have a word with him."

"He needs stopping, Mr Rhea, words are no good. He's behaving illegally, so he is."

"What law is he breaking?" I had been taught a good deal about public service vehicles at Training School and knew sufficient to appreciate that Claude Jeremiah could be running an unlawful public service vehicle. In those days, it was illegal to charge passengers separate fares in private cars, because this brought the car within the realm of a public service vehicle. Besides, ordinary motorcar insurance didn't cover such use so it seemed there'd be an insurance offence too.

I wanted to know if Arnold knew the rules. He did. He promptly reeled off a list of rules and regulations likely to be broken by the enterprising Claude Jeremiah.

"You won't have mentioned this to anyone else, have you?" I put to Arnold.

"No, but I've grumbled a lot, to my passengers, my regulars."

"I was thinking of the Traffic Commissioners," I told him.

"No, should I tell them?" he asked in all innocence.

"They might investigate your affairs too, Arnold — like your carriage of goods for reward . . ."

"Oh." He saw what I was driving at. "Oh, aye, well. I see. Can this be dealt with quietly, Mr Rhea?"

"If I take Claude Jeremiah to court, Arnold, he might hit back at you; he might complain officially to me about your activities, or he might drop an anonymous line to the Traffic Commissioners about the goods-carrying affairs of Merryweather Coaches."

"I am allowed to carry parcels, Mr Rhea, and passengers are allowed to fetch parcels on board, you know."

"I wouldn't classify a hundred dozen eggs as a parcel, Arnold."

"It's serious, Mr Rhea, I am insured, he's not. You'll have a word with him?"

"I will," I promised. "But you should be more careful about carrying parcels, eh?"

In the seclusion of my office, I settled down with my books to refresh my memory on the laws about public service vehicles, or P.S.V.s as we knew them. I knew they fell into three groups — a stage carriage was one which carried passengers at separate fares while not fulfilling the definition of an express carriage. The ordinary town service bus or a rural bus were typical examples. An express carriage was a P.S.V. carrying passengers at separate fares none of which was less than one shilling or some other prescribed greater sum. Long-distance express coaches fitted this definition, like the overnight runs to London or Liverpool. The third was a contract carriage which did not carry passengers at separate fares — like a bus hired to take a party to the theatre or a football match.

The other rules and case law on buses were highly complicated with many exceptions and provisos. I concluded that if Claude Jeremiah was charging his passengers separate fares for their trips he was operating a public service vehicle. The appearance of his vehicle was immaterial. This meant he was

125

breaking umpteen rules of the road, including motor insurance offences, public service vehicle licence offences and a host of others.

The first job was to prove that Claude Jeremiah's old banger was a bus, and that meant catching him with a full load of paying passengers. After having words with Arnold about the most beneficial time to halt Claude's motor, I arranged to position myself one morning on a wide stretch of road at the far boundary of my beat. This was the route taken by Claude Jeremiah, and it was an ideal place to halt a moving vehicle. Furthermore, he would have a full load by the time he reached this place.

Sure enough, soon after quarter past nine, the distant rumble of the ancient car reached my ears as it laboured towards the lofty boundary of Aidensfield beat. I was in full uniform and stepped impressively into the centre of the road as the rattling machinery approached. With a screech of brakes and a multitudinous banging and clattering, the old car groaned to a halt and Claude Jeremiah wound down his window.

"Morning, Mr Rhea." His tiny brown face creased into an uneasy grin as he regarded me from his driving-seat. "Want a lift?"

"Morning, Claude Jeremiah. Full load, eh?" I stooped to peer inside. The car was packed with people and I counted nine heads including the driver. They were chiefly grey-haired ladies, as tight as baby wrens in their nest.

"Aye, just giving some friends a lift into York," he said.

"Do you mind if I have a word with them?" I asked.

"Summat important, is it?" shrilled a woman's voice from inside. "We've a busy day, Mr Policeman. We go like this because it's quicker than yon bus, trundling down farm tracks and the like, delivering eggs and pigs. Mr Greengrass gets us there on time . . ."

"Are you a taxi then?" I asked him.

"No, just a friendly cove giving pals a lift — being community-spirited, in a manner of speaking, Mr Rhea."

"What is the cost of your trip?" I asked the passengers.

"Half a crown apiece," said a woman. "Two bob if you get on at Elsinby."

"Look, Mr Rhea." Claude climbed from his car and stood on the road, facing me. "I'm doing a public service. I can do a return trip cheaper than Merryweather and I get them there quicker. Tell me what's wrong with that."

"By doing what you are doing—" I tried to sound professionally knowledgeable and adopted an official tone— "you are fulfilling the role of a bus. That means you need licensing as a bus. You are therefore operating without the necessary licences. And you are not insured."

"He's doing us a favour, Mr Rhea, giving us a lift. If we decide to tip him a half dollar or pay for the petrol, that's up to us . . ."

"It's not as easy as that, Mrs Prescott," I said. "There are rules to obey and careful safety regulations to follow . . ."

"If an accident happened to any of you in this car," I said, "your families would not get compensation. Claude is not insured for paying passengers — he's running a hell of a risk because he can't afford to pay for your injuries or loss."

"He's a taxi . . .," bellowed a deep-voiced woman from within.

"He's not a taxi, not when he charges separate fares and picks you up at stages, and he's not licensed as a hackney-carriage either. If he wants to do this sort of thing, he could get licensed as a hackney-carriage . . ."

"Look Mr Rhea . . ."

The situation was getting out of hand. By now, all the irate ladies had disembarked and were standing around glaring at me and their voices began to rise with irritation and anger as I pathetically tried to explain the rules and to point out the risks to themselves. But it was futile. No one wanted to know the intricacies of public service vehicle licensing laws — all they wanted was to get into the shops as quickly as possible.

"Right!" I shouted. "Listen to me," and I banged on the roof of the car to emphasise my words.

Silence fell.

"Claude Jeremiah is breaking the law in several ways, and I intend to take action against him," I said sternly. "And if you agree to go along with him in this you are also aiding and abetting him. That means you could all go to court, every one of you."

Their gabbling stopped and now they listened carefully as I explained their liability, but as I talked I heard the approaching music of Arnold's bus. It was heading this way, as I knew it would, and it was making hard work of climbing the hill towards our present position. I kept the women there, talking in graphic detail about the fearsome penalties that could be inflicted upon those who aided and abetted the functioning of illegal buses.

As the bus appeared in view, I told them it would take me an hour to interview Claude Jeremiah about the miscellaneous offences that had been disclosed, and at this juncture the strident voice of Mrs Prescott shouted:

"Claude Jeremiah — give us our money back. We're catching that bus . . ."

"But . . ." He stared at me and then at them.

"It could prevent you going to court," I added slyly.

He began to fumble in his pockets and by this time the bus was upon us. I raised my hand and halted Arnold's onward progress.

"Morning, Arnold. Going to York?"

"Aye, Mr Rhea. Got some passengers for me, have you?"

"There's a few ladies in need of urgent transport to York," I said.

"There's room enough in here," he told me and I climbed in for a look.

"Your aisles are not blocked, I see," I smiled. "No crates of eggs or manacled pigs blocking the exits?"

"No, Mr Rhea, I run a properly conducted public service vehicle."

And I happened to see that all twenty-two passengers had on their knees four or five egg-boxes, all full. A hundred dozen eggs . . .

"All these ladies and gentlemen are taking eggs into York market," he said, smiling at me.

"I don't want to know about their private arrangements." I left the bus and watched Claude's passengers clamber aboard. They paid their fares and with a double hoot of the horn the old bus rumbled on its way.

"That was nasty of you, Mr Rhea," Claude grumbled.

"I've saved you from a fate worse than death!" I countered. "If the Traffic Commissioners had got hold of you, my lad, your feet would never touch the ground. I'm not taking you to court on this occasion, Claude Jeremiah, although I should do so. Regard this as a warning — no more pinching bus passengers. If you want to make money with your car, get yourself licensed as a taxi."

"Yes, Mr Rhea."

He looked dejected, but I think it was for the best. If I'd taken him to court, there would have been a long, involved and highly controversial case about what constitutes a bus, and I was happy to let him go with an unofficial warning.

"Do I need a licence to carry other things then?" he asked me with a crafty gleam in his eyes.

"Other things?" I asked.

"Well, folks keep asking me to deliver things in York, you see . . . carry stuff for them . . ."

I stared at him and said, "Open your boot, Claude Jeremiah."

He gingerly opened it and it was full of cartons of fresh eggs.

"If you convey goods for hire or reward, you need a goods vehicle licence," I informed him. "And you need a special excise licence . . ."

"I'll have to take those back then," he said.

"I haven't seen those, Claude, not today. I might stop and inspect your boot another day . . ."

"Thank you, Mr Rhea, thank you."

He locked the boot, jumped inside his old car and roared away in a cloud of oily fumes.

Perhaps it seemed a little unfair to let Arnold's bus continue to carry eggs, pigs and the like, but Claude was too much of a risk to allow loose upon the public with his car. In his case, people could suffer awful consequences — in Arnold's case, only Arnold could suffer.

If the soft-glove treatment worked on this occasion, I would be pleased, but I wondered how long it would be before we had the Greengrass Taxi Line. A shudder ran down my spine.

\* \* \*

For the next few months I had little contact with Merryweather Coaches and, so far as I know, Arnold never experienced a visitation by the Traffic Commissioners. I felt it unwise to check too closely upon his goods-carrying activities because he did provide a service to isolated rural communities. For Arnold, therefore, business began to boom. Contrary to the national trend, his bus service gathered more and more passengers and he felt obliged to employ a conductress to ease his burden.

He had found that his precious time was being consumed at every stop; he spent many useful minutes issuing tickets or delivering change and reckoned that if he paid for the services of a conductress much time and effort would be saved. Furthermore, his passengers would receive a swifter service. He placed an advert in every post-office window of the district and some eight or nine ladies made rapid application for the post. This was long before the days of the Sex Discrimination Act and it is possible that Arnold envisaged a delightful creature of exceptional beauty parading the length of his coach, but in this sense the sun did not shine on Arnold.

None of the seven hopefuls could even be described as remotely attractive, although five could count money and one knew how to change a wheel. After interviewing each woman, Arnold settled for Miss Hannah Pybus, whose name

130

led to many nicknames aboard the coach. Some of the children called her Fly-Bus or Hannah Wide-Bus, the latter being due to the somewhat extensive measurement of her hips.

Hannah was a spinster of the parish of Thackerston and was in her fifties. She had lived with her retired father for years, never working at a normal job but spending her time looking after the old man. He had died several months ago and she now needed an outlet. The opportunity of a job which took her free of charge into conurbations like Ashfordly and Elsinby, and into that far-off place of York, was a godsend. A whole new world opened for Hannah Pybus.

It was sad that Hannah was not in the least attractive in her appearance. From a distance, there could be considerable doubt as to whether she was male or female, for she was almost six feet tall, with a frame like a battleship and hips like the proverbial rear-end of an African bull elephant. Stout, trunk-like legs supported her massive frame and she walked with a strange, sailor-like motion, as if throwing her body forward in an attempt to keep it mobile. Her shapeless, outdated clothes concealed any semblance of breasts or waistline while her face was heavy about the jowls with sandy-coloured tufts of hair sprouting from all manner of odd places. She had a freckled face with pale brown eyes and a mop of sandy-coloured hair on top, the strands held in place with tortoise-shell slides with a thick red ribbon at the back.

Being a lady of leisure, therefore, she embarked on her new job with characteristic gusto, cycling daily from her cottage at Thackerston to Arnold's depot at Ashfordly, some six or seven miles. Her cycle had a basket on the front and a wire skirt-guard at each side of the rear wheel. Somehow she forced the pedals of her gallant machine to carry her up the long incline to Aidensfield Bank Top before gathering speed for the remaining four-mile run into Ashfordly.

After Arnold had explained the intricacies of his ticket machine and accounting system, he took off for York with Hannah aboard. She was clad in a shapeless gown coloured purple and cream to match his coaching colours and looked like a statue awaiting its unveiling ceremony. In her enthusiasm as the first passenger entered, she pounced on him and demanded his destination. He paid all the way to York, even though he only wanted to go to Elsinby.

Within a week, she was totally in charge. Arnold told me he'd never seen anything like it. Hardly had the last passenger boarded at any given stop, than Hannah rang the bell to send him along his route. There were no delays now. She proceeded to allocate seats to the passengers, leaving them no choice in the matter, and demanded their fares while making sure they behaved. Children quaked when she appeared, old men didn't dare smoke their foul pipes and the village gossips watched their language as Hannah hovered around, eagle-eyed and always anxious to please her boss.

There is little doubt that Arnold and his finances benefited from her presence. He was able to concentrate upon his driving and maintenance, while Hannah cared for the interiors of the two buses. She polished and washed, swept and tidied, and she seldom made an error with the cash. The general behaviour of passengers, especially children and drunks, improved tremendously and the net result was that more people used Merryweather Coaches. They seemed happy to obey Hannah when on board. Arnold was in his sixth heaven and, whenever I saw him in the Brewers Arms, he talked incessantly of bus-conductresses, buses and bus routes. For him, Hannah provided a new dimension in his life, but for the regulars in the pub they grew just as sick of Hannah as they did with every other facet of bus-lore. Even so, they all agreed that it was nice to see Arnold so happy.

There was even talk of a romance between the unlikely pair, although it was universally agreed that the man who took Hannah in all her prime showed gallantry of the highest order or foolishness of the most awful kind. Nothing developed along those lines while I was at Aidensfield, although I did note Arnold's starry eyes as he talked about Hannah's role in his coaching enterprise. Maybe there was something there? Maybe he did drive her home after the last trip, with her cycle in the rear and his hands on the wheel?

It is quite true to say that the entire community was delighted at the success of Arnold's venture. The little bus company with its huge conductress did a roaring trade and Hannah did allow some parcels to be carried. She had studied the *Conduct of Drivers, Conductors and Passengers Regulations 1936 and 1946*, consequently she knew which goods were permitted and which had never to be brought aboard. She knew that she must never talk to the driver when driving, unless for safety reasons, and she appreciated that it was her duty to enforce the regulations relating to the conduct of passengers, and to see that the route, fare and destination notices were properly displayed.

Hannah enforced the rules most carefully. She enforced those which said passengers had not to be disorderly, that they had to enter and alight in the correct manner and not through skylights or windows, that they had not to distract the driver's attention, nor distribute notices or advertising matter aboard the bus. She had learned that they must not play noisy instruments or throw bottles, coins and litter about the place, nor allow any banners, flags or streamers to overhang the road outside. She made sure they did not soil the vehicle or be offensive, either in behaviour or clothing. Loaded firearms had not to be taken on board, nor had any other offensive article and no one could bring an animal aboard without the consent of an authorised person. Hannah reckoned she was authorised to refuse the pigs, lambs, hens and goats although she did tolerate such creatures if the accompanying adult would clean up the mess and keep the creature under control.

Hannah knew that she had wide powers to enforce the observance of these rules, and that a constable was also given like powers. If any passenger contravened the regulations, he had to give his name and address on demand to the driver or conductor, or to a constable, and such a person could be removed from the bus by either the driver or the conductor, or by a constable if requested by those officials.

It was difficult to envisage an occasion when I would be called to act officially, for I knew Hannah would quell any riot by the merest glance of those pale eyes, but one Wednesday afternoon I found myself involved in what appeared to be an infringement of the *Conduct of Drivers, Conductors and Passengers Regulations*.

I was in my office at home, writing reports, when Arnold's bus halted outside and a very distraught Hannah hurried down the path. I opened the door to admit her, for she was clearly distressed. I gathered from her first words that a passenger had infringed the rules in a rather peculiar way.

"Calm down, Hannah!" I said. "Take a deep breath and then tell me about it."

She took a huge breath, enough to drain a hot-air balloon, and her colossal bosom swelled behind my counter and threatened to dislodge the typewriter. But the trick worked, for her face lost its initial look of horror and disgust, and she sighed.

"By Jove, Mr Rhea, it was a nasty shock, I can tell you."

"Come in and sit down." I lifted the flap on the office counter and invited her in for a seat. She settled down and refused a cup of tea; Arnold was waiting outside in the bus and would take her home. She'd give him a cup in her house and would have hers then. He wouldn't come in, she said, as he found it all too embarrassing.

"So what happened on that bus?" I asked.

She swallowed hard and I could see she was acutely embarrassed.

"It was a man," she said. "He . . . er . . . well, he broke the rules about the conduct of passengers . . . he was offensive," she added quickly.

"Dirty clothing? Been cleaning out his pigs, had he?"

"No," she said, gritting her teeth. "It was worse than that, Mr Rhea, much, much worse."

"Go on, I must know what he did if I am to take action."

She swallowed again.

I waited.

"He . . . look, Mr Rhea, I'm not very good at explaining things . . ."

"I'm good at listening," I assured her. "Take your time."

She paused, clearly trying to select the right words to describe her ordeal, and all the time my curiosity was increasing. What on earth had happened aboard Merryweather Coaches to create such an effect upon the redoubtable Hannah Pybus?

"He was indecent." She managed to spit out the word.

"Indecent?" I asked. "How? Did he swear at you?"

She shook that pale gingery head.

"No, it was worse than that. I'm not fussy about a swear-word or two, Mr Rhea. This was worse than any swear-word."

"Go on." I was getting interested now. Had he taken a grab at her? Some passengers weren't slow in smacking the shapely bottoms of conductresses, but I couldn't imagine anyone being so fuddled as to smack Hannah's spacious rump regions. Maybe a drunken passenger had done that, or seized her by some other part of her towering frame? The thought was astonishing.

"He exposed himself at me." She lowered her head and blushed furiously as the words emerged.

"Indecent exposure?" I asked. "On a bus?"

"Yes," she said, relaxing now she had clarified the situation.

Immediately, my Training School knowledge began to click within the farmost regions of my mind. Indecent exposure was a public nuisance if it was done *publicly*. If Hannah alone had seen the object in question, it might not be an indictable common law offence. There being no public viewing. The Vagrancy Act, 1824, section 4, offered a possible solution because it created a summary offence for a man to wilfully, openly, lewdly and obscenely expose the person with intent to insult a female. Nothing said what "the person" meant here, but most of us had a good idea. If the fellow

135

intended to insult Hannah, that provision might fit the circumstances. The Town Police Clauses Act 1847 also created an offence of indecent exposure if it occurred in any street to the annoyance of residents or passengers. Arnold's bus wasn't a street, so I had to rule out the latter offence. Because the Common Law offence must be proved to be a *public* display I was left with the Vagrancy Act and its quaint Victorian phraseology.

On a bus? I knew there were no buses when the Vagrancy Act came into force, but happily that old law, still in force, left the situation sufficiently open to cater for such crimes. Besides, the *Conduct of Drivers, Conductors and Passengers Regulations of 1936* and *1946* would cope with the fellow, if all else failed. I felt I could proceed with the matter.

"An indecent exposure on a bus, Hannah. Would you say you were insulted?" I had to ask this in order to prove the case, should it ever reach court. It was part of the Victorian wording of the statute.

"Insulted! I was mortified!" she said, hurt at my question.

"I have to ask, as it's an essential ingredient of the offence. The lady must be insulted if I am to take action."

"I was grossly insulted!" she stressed.

With her use of words like this, I was reminded of the police recruit who defined Gross Indecency as "Indecency between a large number of persons, 144, I think".

"Who was the man?" I asked next.

"I don't know his name, but he got on at York. He was all right until I went for his fare. He got off at that lane end, just before you get into Elsinby from York."

"You'd know him again?"

She nodded. "Oh yes, I'd know him again!"

"Did you tell anyone at the time?"

"No, I didn't want to upset the passengers. I told Arnold when we got to the terminus and he said I'd better mention it to you."

"Certainly. Well, it looks as if he lives on my beat. What's he like?"

She described a man about fifty years old, with grey hair and an unshaven appearance. He was a small man, she said, wearing a dirty raincoat and heavy black boots. All flashers wore dirty raincoats, I thought. This one fitted the traditional pattern.

Having described him quite well, I had to ask her precisely what he had done. It was important from the prosecution point of view.

She blushed furiously once again and asked, "Do I really have to tell you?"

"I'm afraid so. I must know precisely what he did, Hannah, if I'm to take any action."

"Well," she said. "Er . . . his trousers front was open and . . . it . . . his thing . . . it was sticking right out."

"Did he draw your attention to it?"

"Yes, he did!" she snapped.

"How?" I asked.

"He placed his fare on it, for me to take."

"His fare?" I almost doubled up with laughter at this latest technique, but managed to keep a straight face.

"Yes, he spread the money out, right along it."

"And how much was his fare?"

"A shilling," she said. "He laid it out, right along his thing."

"What sort of coins were they?" I was fascinated now.

"Pennies," she said calmly. "Twelve pennies."

My mind boggled. Side by side, they'd cover a large area, but twelve £.s.d. pennies laid out in a line covered an enormous distance, nearly fifteen inches. I made her repeat this. I had to be sure I got it right. Who was this man, I wondered? It looked as if we had a world record-breaker in the locality.

"And?" I asked.

"Well, I refused to accept them . . ." she said pertly. "I made him collect them himself and pay his fare."

"And did he?"

"Yes, he did!"

"And then he put it away?"

"I don't know. He was all alone on the back seat and I didn't stay a minute longer."

If my report of this event reached Force Headquarters, the place would be in uproar and every member of the police service would be jealous. I could imagine a stampede to check the veracity of this claim, but one's constabulary duty must be done.

"Thanks, Hannah. I'll make enquiries and I'll let you know how I get on. You go home now and have that cup of tea with Arnold."

She left the office and, as the bus rumbled out of sight I collapsed in a fit of laughter. I'd never heard anything like this before and felt sure Hannah had made a mistake. What had she seen? I racked my brains to identify the fellow and then I realised who it was.

Poor Hannah!

But, first, I had to check my theory. I jumped aboard the little Francis Barnett and chugged over the valley to Elsinby. Through the village, I turned left along a rough lane until I arrived at Bankside Cottage. I knocked, for I knew old Bill Firby was at home. Smoke was rising from his chimney. Soon the green door was opened and Bill stood there, his jacket open and his face registering surprise when he saw me.

"Hello, Mr Rhea." He stood back to invite me in. "You're a stranger at my door."

"Aye," I agreed, entering his cosy home. "It's not often I have cause to call on you."

"Summat up, is it?" He led me into his sitting-room where a cosy fire burned, and pointed to an armchair. I settled with my crash-helmet on my lap.

"Bill, you're going to laugh when I've finished this tale, but I need your answers first. Were you on the bus out of York today?"

"Aye," he said. "Yes, I was."

"And Hannah was conductress?"

"She was."

"And did you pay your fare all in pennies?"

"Aye, I hadn't a shilling piece, so I used pennies. Nowt wrong with that, is there?"

"No, there isn't." I laughed now. "You've cleared up a massive problem for me."

"I have?"

The truth was that Bill had only one hand. His left hand was missing at the wrist, and that arm terminated in an irregular fleshy stump. He wore no covering and no false hand. On the bus, his fare had been in his right-hand pocket and in order to count it he had pulled up his left sleeve to expose his arm from his elbow down to his wrist. To gain stability for his stump, he had placed his elbow on his lap, tucking it firmly into his groin, and he rested his wrist on his right leg. He had then laid out the coins for Hannah to count, placing them along his arm.

Hannah, poor unmarried woman, had totally misunderstood this innocent action.

When I told him the essence of her complaint, he laughed until tears rolled down his eyes and asked if I was going to tell her the truth.

"Yes, of course," I assured him.

"Nay, lad, don't do that. Think of my reputation if she spreads that tale around. I'll be the envy of all the blokes for miles around!"

But I had to tell Hannah the truth. I did and she listened intently; happily, she laughed when I explained Bill's fare-paying technique. Whenever he travelled by bus or paid in a shop, he always used that system, I explained.

"Oh," she said. "Silly of me. I'm sorry to have troubled you Mr Rhea. I will apologise to Mr Firby when I see him."

"He's not worried," I said. "There's no need to bother yourself any more about it."

"Thank you, Mr Rhea," she beamed and I left her comfortable house.

On reflection, that little episode raised more questions about Hannah's past than it solved. Until then, we had assumed she had never had a man friend, but perhaps she had.

We all wondered who it might have been.

# CHAPTER SEVEN

Crabbed age and youth cannot live together;
Youth is full of pleasance, age is full of care.
WILLIAM SHAKESPEARE,
1564–1616, *The Passionate Pilgrim*

It has been said that the duties of a police officer do not include social work. In theory, there are skilled professionals to undertake such responsibilities, but in practice the work of a police officer does include a whole range of jobs which could be classified as social work. The conscientious constable visits the sick, the lame, the infirm and the aged because one of his basic functions is to protect life and property. If he can call upon those in need of help, he might save a life or prevent damage to property. His presence is often reassuring to the lonely and frightened.

The rural bobby in particular spends a good deal of his time, on and off duty, visiting the aged upon his beat. I was no exception.

During my daily tour I would drop in, unannounced, upon many pensioners and have a cup of tea with them. I think Sergeant Blaketon frowned upon this; he never said so because I had pre-empted any criticism from him by stressing that I considered this to be an important part of a rural constable's work. He suffered my cups of tea in silence and I got the impression he resented my free tea rather than the time I spent indoors chatting for no apparent constabulary purpose. Sergeant Blaketon was one of the old school; he liked policemen to be seen and he liked them to be always asking questions about unsolved crimes or seeking criminal information from likely sources. He failed to appreciate the very basic social requirements of the job.

While law-enforcement is a vital part of the constable's task, it is no more important than the welfare of those under the constable's care, and I made certain he knew how I felt.

Gradually, I learned of the whereabouts of the lonely aged on my patch; I was not too concerned about those who lived with their families, or even those with families living nearby. I needed to know about the widowed and lonely, the isolated person with no relatives to call upon. These were my concern — they might be suffering from illness, or they might have fallen and hurt themselves; they might be plagued by stupid vandals or be the butt of confidence tricksters . . . all kinds of social evils can befall an elderly person living alone and I wanted no villainy against those residing on my beat.

Visiting these marvellous old folks was a wonderful experience. There was a man of ninety-two who had made ornamental buttons for Queen Victoria; a lady of eighty-seven who recalled seeing Queen Victoria when she visited the district in 1900 and a man of eighty-three who fell down an apple-tree and who pleaded me not to tell his wife how he'd hurt his back. I liked the man of eighty-eight who was ill and, when I asked if he wanted me to tell anyone, he asked me to notify his schoolteacher, a Miss Wilkinson. She'd taught him as a boy in primary school and, thinking he was senile, I checked — she was still alive and enjoying the sunshine in Eltering, aged 98!

Yorkshire folk are noted for their contemptuous attitude to old age. It is merely a nuisance to them, something like a nagging illness. No self-respecting Yorkshireman will admit to being ill. They fight illness by pretending it doesn't exist, and will continue working through ailments that would fell lesser mortals.

This stubborn attitude is shown in a lovely tale about a young lady newspaper reporter who called to see a Yorkshire villager. He had reached 100 years of age and was inside his house as the reporter talked to his daughter.

"You must be very proud of your father," the reporter commented.

"Oh, Ah don't know," replied his daughter. "He's done nowt but grow old, and look how long it's taken him to do that!"

The elderly crack jokes among themselves, such as "Awd Sam's refusing to die because it saves funeral expenses", while another in his nineties commented, "When Ah was a lad, Ah used to get oot o' bed ivvery morning at five, but now Ah's gittin on a bit, it's very near six before Ah stir."

Those with a literary turn of mind might consider the words written by the poet Edward Spenser which so aptly sum up the feeling of creeping senility. He wrote:

The careful cold hath nipt my rugged rind,
And in my face deep furrows old hath plight;
My head besprent with hoary frost I find,
And by mine eyes the crow his claw doth wright;
Delight is laid about and pleasure past;
No sun now shines, clouds have all over-cast.

One wonders what he knew about old age, because he died in 1599 at the ripe old age of 46.

In reality, however, I found the aged had minds of their own. Their opinions, which had been nurtured over many generations, were so firmly established that no amount of argument or discussion would shift them. I had to accept this as a fact of life. Change is not welcome in the land of the aged. Memories of loved ones do feature in this tough, inflexible attitude and can lead to a softening manner or even a change of opinion. Such a case involved old Mrs Ada Flanagan of Aidensfield and her easy-chair.

* * *

The chair was nothing special to look at. It was of simple design and rather old-fashioned for it had wings at the back and castors beneath which squeaked every time it moved. The upholstery was dull grey but this lack of glamour was concealed by a faded cover of deep-blue material, offset with a floral design. Mrs Flanagan had made the covers herself some ten or fifteen years ago and was undoubtedly proud of her handicraft. She called it Bill's chair.

That the chair needed a new cover was obvious to me, but I sensed it was imprudent to even suggest it. Although she'd asked me not to sit in that chair, I think she welcomed my visits for she would make me a cup of tea when I called, usually around eleven o'clock on a morning. In respect for her wishes, I would never sit in that chair to drink it, always using a dining-chair at the table. Bill's chair was always in the same position, I noticed, just to the right of the fireside. There it was close enough to the mantelpiece for Old Bill to have reached out for his pipe or tobacco, or his racing papers.

Through those regular visits, I learned all about Bill's chair. He had occupied it every evening after work and in retirement had used it during the day as well. He liked it exactly where it now stood, and she was determined that it should remain there.

I whiled away many hours drinking Mrs Flanagan's tea and listening to her constant chatter as she either ironed or baked on the table before me.

She would talk about her childhood in Ireland and how she went potato-picking on her father's farm. I knew it had been a struggle to earn a living; then, when she was twenty, she had married Bill Flanagan. He'd always wanted to go to Scotland — and so he had, with his young wife.

That old chair had been one of their first possessions as man and wife. Sometimes she would laugh as she told me how they would both use it — they would sit in it together because they had nothing else! She would sit on Bill's knee and they'd chat together as only a young couple can; this chair had been their joy until they could afford more furniture.

In Scotland, their fortunes had improved and Bill had found a good job on a farm; gradually they built their little home, with this chair always occupying the prime position near the fireside.

As my first year as the village bobby passed, it seemed as if I was an old friend to Mrs Flanagan. Perhaps I was because I knew all about her wishes, hopes, sadnesses and past history. We knew each other very well, I felt. I also felt I knew Old Bill; although he'd died long before I came to Aidensfield, her stories had made him live anew. Sometimes I could almost see him in that battered old chair, so vivid were her memories.

Then, quite unexpectedly, Mrs Flanagan started to go out to work. I was quite surprised, but she told me she did this to occupy herself and to earn a few coppers. Her new part-time job was to cover chairs and furniture, or make curtains. She told me she used to do that sort of work when she was younger but in those days her skills had been confined to the family or for the benefit of close friends. She'd never thought about doing it professionally, but had seen an advert in the local paper.

It had been placed by a department store in Ashfordly who sought a seamstress capable of covering chairs and making curtains on a part-time basis. The work entailed some travelling to take measurements in the homes of customers, all of whom lived locally, while the actual sewing could be done at the seamstress's home.

For Mrs Flanagan it was the ideal job and she was appointed. I could see it was the making of her.

Then, quite suddenly, I noticed the chair had gone. One morning as I called, I could see that Old Bill's chair was no longer before the hearth and in its place was a modern chair with slender wooden arms. I'd seen this one before, in Mrs Flanagan's front room when I'd been in for sherry and Christmas cake.

So from that day forward I sat in that new chair for my cups of tea, but I didn't dare ask the whereabouts of the old blue one. Perhaps some bygone memory had upset her? I didn't dare risk an upset by referring to it, so left my questions unasked.

Nowadays she chatted to me and made my usual cups of tea as she told me of the people she met during her travels and how nice they all were. She used the buses, or a taxi if it was urgent, and I knew the job had given her a new lease of life.

Sometimes I found her ironing chair-covers and curtains as well as her own washing. But I still wondered what had happened to Old Bill's chair?

Where had it gone? Why had she moved it? It was really no concern of mine although I often felt like asking about it. Maybe it was linked with her acceptance of this job? But I never asked.

Then one summer morning, I called as usual but she didn't hear me enter. I had knocked and walked in like I always did, but she was busy in the front room. I could hear her old but efficient sewing-machine whirring away, so I stepped across the floor to tap on the front room door.

She stopped her work; the door opened and I saw the old treadle machine with yards of material strewn about it. She had a mouth full of pins and the floor was covered with paper patterns and cut pieces. I was surprised to see such a large amount of cloth but I was equally surprised to notice the material was the same colour and pattern as that battered old cover on Bill's chair. Was she covering his chair? Here was a new design, an exact copy of that old one, but all this material for one chair?

She smiled as I entered and took the pins out of her mouth.

"Go and sit down," she said. "I've got to finish this edge and I'll be through."

"Don't rush and spoil it," I told her. "I'll make the tea!"

Her quiet smile told me that this was a good idea, so I left her to continue her work. I knew where everything was and before long had the kettle boiling. When I made the tea she came to join me and brought a length of cloth which she hand-stitched as we chatted.

We talked about the weather, the news, the village problems and a young couple down the road who were expecting their first child. Occasionally we lapsed into silence as she came to a tricky part of her work; throughout, I watched her quietly.

In some ways, my time in her house was like stepping back half a century — there were the worn beams, the ponderous tick of the grandfather clock, the black-leaded iron grate and its glowing fire which invariably crackled and spat with logs newly cut. The brasses shone and the windows glittered after years of methodic housework.

I enjoyed the peace and atmosphere of this place. Mrs Flanagan had captured the slow-moving rhythm of her life and her mode of existence was the epitome of country life. I liked it.

"You know," I spoke after a spell of silence, "I'd miss this cup of tea and chat, Mrs Flanagan. I really look forward to it. I'm pleased you don't work full-time."

"So am I," she said, "and it's nice to talk to somebody who doesn't pass on everything I say!"

These confidences were clearly something she treasured and yet we had never reached the Christian-name stage. I always called her Mrs Flanagan and would no more dream of using her first name than she would of using mine. We were friends but kept our distance and our chats were confined to these occasional visits. Maybe that's why our talks were so successful — in some way, I was like one of those anonymous people who answer letters and give advice in magazines and newspaper columns. I was someone she could trust with her innermost thoughts and I knew we had a fine platonic relationship and eventually I knew that I could safely broach the subject of Old Bill's chair, more so because she was working with material which was an exact replica of that which covered his absent fireside friend.

"That's nice material." I pointed to the piece in her hands. "Is it an urgent job?"

"For the weekend," she answered. "The van is coming for it on Friday afternoon. It's for a young couple over at Fernley. Their parents gave them an old three-piece suite to start their home and they wanted it covering. It'll look nice when it's finished — it's a real good suite, you know. One of the type which seem to last for ever."

"They made things to last in those days," I said.

She nodded and there was another pause.

"It's exactly the same as the pattern on Bill's chair," I spoke slowly.

Perhaps I shouldn't have said it! Immediately the words were out, I regretted having said them. But I needn't have worried.

"I know," she spoke quietly. "It's funny really. Here I am, covering furniture for a young couple with material which is exactly the same I used for our first chair — the very first bit of furniture we had, me and Bill."

There was no finer moment to ask about Old Bill's chair.

"Where is his chair, Mrs Flanagan? You haven't sold it, have you?"

She shook her head. "It's upstairs, in the spare room."

"I liked that chair," I told her. "It looked so comfy and warm."

"It was Bill's," she said simply.

I didn't answer. Perhaps she didn't want to talk about it anymore, and that last brief sentence told me everything. Because it was Bill's, she wouldn't want to give it away or sell it, and yet for the same reason she wouldn't want it in this room where it would constantly remind her of his absence, especially when others tried to sit in it.

But she was talking again.

"I always wanted to cover it for him," she was saying. "I did it years ago and he liked it so much that he didn't want any other pattern on it."

"It was nice," I said briefly.

She was in full flow now. "It became very shabby, you know. He would sit in it after work, often in his working clothes and it got awfully dirty. I washed the covers time and time again to try and keep them fresh-looking."

"It was always nice when I came," I added.

"Yes, but it was so worn, wasn't it? Faded and threadbare."

"And he didn't want another cover! Was that why you moved it, because it was getting shabby?"

She shook her head. "No, not really. It was my Bill's chair, you see. He didn't want me to touch it — he loved it just as it was, you understand. Well, if I'd had it in this room, I'd be itching to re-cover it. And Bill wouldn't want that."

"So you put it out of temptation's way?"

"Yes. I wouldn't part with it, not for the world, so the spare bedroom was the best place. I use it sometimes myself, when I'm dusting upstairs. I use it to have a sit down, you understand, and it gets dusted regularly."

"Why didn't he want it re-covering?" I asked, feeling that we could talk freely.

"He didn't tell me."

"Can't you guess?"

"I think I can," she answered slowly. "I covered that chair specially for him. He found the material in a shop years and years ago, and it was just what he wanted. He grew attached to it — he wasn't a fellow for changing things without good reason."

"I know," I sympathised, "men get like that. But you could cover it now, couldn't you?"

"Do you really think so?" Her eyes sparkled with new interest and I knew she'd been wanting someone to say that.

"With this new material," I continued. "It's exactly the same as Bill's chair — he would love that, wouldn't he?"

"It's just what he always wanted," she whispered. "We looked in all the shops for this colour but never found it. Not in all our years. All the shops said it was too old-fashioned and out of stock."

"That was a few years ago," I reminded her. "And now that same pattern is right in fashion again. That often happens — I know Bill would agree now, wouldn't he?"

"Thank you," for her only reply, and I rose to leave, then she said, "Would you like to see the finished covers?"

Puzzled, I followed her into the workroom and there I saw a fourth cover, shaped differently from the rest, and admired the style and loving workmanship it contained. When I called the next time, Old Bill's chair was back in its place before the fire, looking regal and splendid in its new cover.

It was a perfect complement to this room.

"I'll make the tea now," she said. "You sit there."

And she pointed to Old Bill's chair.

\* \* \*

One of my favourite characters was Simon Rawlings, a gentleman of eighty-seven who lived with his daughter in a tiny cottage at Elsinby. Tall and erect, he had a guardsman's figure and even though his broad back was stooped with his great age he always tried to walk upright. It was a display of his deep personal pride.

Awd Simon, as the village knew him, was a retired railwayman. He had retired 22 years ago, long before the railways were nationalised, and lived quietly, his wife having been dead nine or ten years. Awd Simon passed his time by gardening and enjoying a pipe of tobacco, plus the occasional pint in the Hopbind Inn. For his age, he was impressive to behold. A good six feet tall, he must have weighed seventeen stone and was built like an ox. The village was full of stories of his young strength, but he was a gentle giant with a lovely touch of humour and a kind word for everyone and everything, man and animal alike.

I got to know him because he spent some sunny afternoons on the seat near the War Memorial and I made myself known to him very early in my period at Aidensfield. I quickly discovered he still lived for the railways, but not the modern diesel engines with their rows of anonymous coaches and hooting horns. Awd Simon worshipped the lovely polished green of the LNER and the maroon livery of the LMS, the romantic days of steam and high-quality service.

As I got acquainted with him, I found it easy to get him reminiscing about his time with the London and North Eastern Railway Company, where he'd worked his way up from track maintenance to fireman, and he'd even been a guard. He told me of the beautiful engines with their own names and distinctive personalities; coaches with splendid first-class compartments and brass fittings. There were pictures of landscapes to interest the passengers and it was essential that the timetables be maintained at all costs. Fear of competition from the maroon giants of the London Midland and Scottish Railway was always present and the company served its customers as a faithful servant would obey his master. Everything had to be right. Second-best would not be tolerated.

He told me about the coal fires in the waiting-rooms, the huge watering-tanks for engines to take on supplies, and the gorgeous floral gardens of the rural stations as they competed for the annual Best-Kept Station prize. Awd Simon would talk for hours about his days with steam-trains and he clearly exuded pride at his part in the history of the railways of this region. He had once seen the Flying Scotsman in Elsinby Station and had actually been on the footplate, the purpose of its visit being a publicity venture in the region. The Mallard too with its distinctive shape had come this way, and he'd seen the King aboard the Royal Train parked overnight in one of the sidings near Elsinby Station.

I often wish I'd written down everything he told me; he was a fund of historic knowledge while his anecdotes and love of the LNER were nothing short of phenomenal.

He had no time for the nationalised British Railways; the stations had become seedy and grimy and no one bothered to light the fires any more. The trains were grubby too, and it was soon after nationalisation that they turned to diesel engines which weren't any better than buses and couldn't cope with the deep snows of the moorland lines. The contrast for Best-Kept Station had ended and all the stations became areas of weeds and overgrown rubbish. Paintwork was allowed to deteriorate and then they began to close the stations. One by one, the rural lines ended . . .

During my conversations with Awd Simon, the process of rural closure was underway. Many branch lines in the north had closed and stations lay derelict in many areas. The newspapers were full of the story, with cries about rural communities being deprived of their lifelines. Some of the villages were so hilly and isolated that no bus company would risk its vehicles on the steep hills or narrow twisting roads. The public joined the general outcry, but the wheels of a determined government were not to be halted. More lines would close; more jobs would be lost and more rural districts would suffer.

No one ever thought this could happen to Elsinby. The busy little station must have paid its way because the locals used the rail service to commute to York or to go shopping to Leeds. They went off to Scarborough or Whitby for the day while the truly adventurous travelled to London and other distant cities. Even though the trains were now drawn by diesel locomotives and bore the British Rail insignia, they were used frequently by the public of Elsinby and district. With its coal business too, the station surely paid its way.

The tiny station, with its signal-box, level-crossing and two platforms was beautiful to behold, for the station-master, a Mr Benjamin Page, made sure it was maintained in an immaculate condition. He boasted white-washed platform front edges, clean oil-lamps, painted seats and offices, a glowing fire in the waiting-room and flowers to adorn the brickwork. For Awd Simon, this was a haven of comfort and he spent many happy hours helping about the station. Mr Page welcomed his presence — he left the responsibility for the appearance of the station in the hands of Awd Simon who weeded between the lines, watered the potted plants, cleaned windows and kept the place at its traditional peak of cleanliness and beauty. Mr Page made good use of Awd Simon.

And then the axe fell. Elsinby Station and the entire branch line through here via Maddleskirk to Thirsk was to be closed. Every possible avenue of reprieve had been examined, and every attempt made to keep the line, but the decision had been made by Parliament. Elsinby Station would close.

Awd Simon blamed the inefficiency of the nationalised system, saying no one had had any heart in the job right from the start. No one cared. For a long time, he looked pale and drawn and, during my regular chats with him on the seat, he was a picture of misery. He could not visualise life without his beloved railway line and the one bright spot was Mr Page's thoughtfulness towards the old man.

He gave him souvenirs, objects which would disappear once the line closed for ever. I know that Simon treasured his square-based oil-lamp from one of the platform lights, the seat with "Elsinby" written across the back and several small items from the booking-office, like a ticket, a pass, a book of rules and so forth.

With his little collection of railway souvenirs, Awd Simon looked rejuvenated. His colour returned, his zest for life reappeared and his general outlook seemed infinitely more hopeful. Even though the line was not reprieved he appeared to have accepted the inevitable. He spent less time around the station although he continued to regale me with the tales of his beloved green engines and the LNER. I was no longer bothered about his health. Awd Simon had accepted that life must go on, and that changes must occur.

I thought no more about his love for the vanishing railway until firm news came of the closure date. It was to be one Friday morning in September.

On that day, the last train would run along our branch line. It would call at all the stations *en route* as it travelled from York via Scarborough, and then through Ryedale via Eltering, Brantsford, Ashfordly, Crampton, Ploatby Junction, Elsinby, Maddleskirk, and eventually into Thirsk where it would join the main London-Edinburgh line for its return journey to York. Passengers would be carried and souvenir tickets would be issued. There would be a restaurant car on the train, with other entertainment, and the sad occasion would be made memorable.

Not wishing to miss any chance of a celebratory occasion, the regulars of the Hopbind Inn at Elsinby formed a committee to arrange suitable festivities in the village. The railway station was to be the focal point and Mr Page agreed. I was duly informed and assured the committee I would attend in my official capacity to control crowds and direct traffic.

What would normally have been a sad occasion for Elsinby became a festive one and I admired the stalwarts of this place for their ability to turn any affair, however sad, into something exciting and enjoyable. For the next few weeks, the place was alive with industry and ideas. I was pleased to see that Awd Simon had been drawn into the arrangements and he was given the special task of informing the new generation about the merits of LNER, LMS, GWR and all the other great rail names of bygone times. He identified engines on postcards and in books, he told historians how they operated and how much coal and water they used . . . notes were made, publicity brochures were printed and, in all, Elsinby was going to lose its station and trains in a blaze of local glory.

When the day came, I motorcycled into Elsinby and parked my Francis Barnett behind the pub, where I left my crash-helmet and motorcycle gear. I donned my regulation-issue flat cap and walked towards the station. Although the last train was not due to pass through until 12.35 p.m., the place was alive with colour and gaiety at 11 o'clock. It seemed that half the village population was already present, few of whom were to travel on the last train. True Elsiners preferred to attend their own celebrations rather than joyride with strangers.

I remember that I was suddenly very busy. Somehow I was inveigled into the last-minute organising and it seemed that everyone had a job of some kind. Then quite suddenly it was twelve noon. There were thirty-five minutes to go, if the train was on time.

Everyone was now on the platform; cars were neatly parked, the pub had shut for the occasion, although George did manage to arrange a makeshift bar in the waiting-room, and everyone queued on the twin platforms. I looked around the gathering, smiling at the young faces, the middle-aged ones and the elderly, all with memories and personal impressions. For the children, it was the start of a new era; for the old, the end of a bygone style of life.

Then I realised I hadn't seen Awd Simon. I thought about it — I'd been here since 11 o'clock and had not once set eyes on the old fellow. I wondered how he was feeling — maybe he'd gone to another station to secure the final ride into Elsinby? Or maybe he was at home, sad and moist-eyed at the thought of this final chapter of his life? Perhaps the emotion was too great, too overpowering, for him to face among crowds?

I was not unduly worried, but when I saw his daughter, Jane, on the up-platform I asked.

"Your dad's not here then?"

"He's somewhere about, Mr Rhea," she smiled. "He said he was working, helping out, and got dressed up in his old clothes."

"Old clothes?" I asked.

"Yes, his railway clothes. You know, his flat cap with a peak, his railway coat and boots. He wore them years ago and never got rid of them. And he took his bait bag with his sandwiches and flask. He got done up in those and said it was something special."

I smiled. Someone had clearly asked a special favour of Awd Simon and, knowing how the committee of the Hopbind functioned, I guessed it would be some set piece for him to perform, some final act and some positive way of making Simon feel needed and useful. I knew, and I'm sure they knew, he'd never see another railway train after today.

Prompt at 12.35 p.m., the diesel with its garlands and gleaming bodywork rumbled into Elsinby Station. It hooted and hooted; the people cheered and several disembarked. Others climbed aboard, there were photographs and singing, paper chains were thrown and flowers tossed at the engine. Photographs were taken as the driver kissed several pretty girls on the platform and the guard did likewise, even including some grannies. It was a glorious ten minutes, and then with a long hoot on the horn the last train from Elsinby drew out of the little station.

Now there were tears. Many spectators, men and women, wept as the full stop was written at the end of this important chapter. Suddenly, and with remarkable simplicity, it was all over. No more trains would pass this way. For over a century, they had used this bonny little station and it had ended so suddenly. It all seemed so unreal. Later the rails would be lifted, the station closed and all its contents disposed of. No longer would the signal cabin be required and the level-crossing gates could be left permanently open for road traffic. No more children would have to be warned of trains and those who wished to shop in York or Leeds would have to find alternative transport.

We all walked away feeling sad, but luckily the bar was open on the station and almost everyone drifted inside for sandwiches. The liquor and food would dispel the feeling of melancholy. I looked around but failed to locate Awd Simon.

"Have you seen Awd Simon?" I asked several people and all shook their heads.

Between one o'clock and three, the celebrations continued and I left the noisy bunch to have a walk around the
village. Away from the station, it was strangely silent, almost
like a village after a funeral. I sought Awd Simon, but failed
to find him. I tried all his pals and all his haunts with no
success. I couldn't understand it at all.

I returned to the festivities and found his daughter, but
she hadn't seen him. She told me he'd been very secretive
about his proposed trip, and not in the least morbid or sad.
He seemed elated, she told me, and she guessed he was doing
something confidential and very personal.

I must admit I felt worried. No one else appeared to be in
the least concerned about his whereabouts, but I felt it odd that
the old man had not taken part in the celebrations. He had certainly dressed up for something connected with today's events.

I went home about four o'clock and had tea with Mary
and the children. They had attended the festivities, albeit not
at Elsinby. They'd been with friends from Aidensfield and
had gone down to Ploatby Junction to see the manoeuvres of
the engine as it transferred itself from one end of the train to
the other for the rest of the trip. The children had secured a
grandstand view from a field near the line and I was pleased
they'd been present on this historic date, even though they'd
probably never remember it in adult life.

I told Mary about Awd Simon but she could shed no
light on his behaviour and had not seen him at Ploatby. After
tea, I changed into my civilian clothes, for I was off duty at
five, and we watched the television news of the train's final
trip. People had turned out right along the route through
Ryedale and made it a colourful and emotional occasion.

At half past seven, the telephone rang and Mary
answered it.

"It's for you," she said. "I said you were off duty and
she should ring Ashfordly, but she insisted she talks to you."

"Who is it?"

"Mrs Jobling."

"Awd Simon's daughter?"

Mary nodded and I went to take the call.

"It's Jane, Mr Rhea," she gasped into the telephone. "It's my dad, he's still not come home. I'm worried now. We've been all over the village and Mr Rawlings says he didn't buy a ticket to go to York or anywhere . . ."

"I'll come right away," I promised.

I spent an hour seeking him in the village, asking members of the committee and everyone else, but no one had seen him. He'd left home this morning in his old railway clothes and had not been seen since. He'd vanished completely.

My professional problem was whether to mount a full-scale police search for the old man, or wait in the hope he'd return home. We had no real reason to think he was lying hurt anywhere, but my instinct told me something was wrong. I began to fear the worst.

I went into the pub and hailed George.

"George." I talked quietly over the counter in the passage. "It's Awd Simon."

"Aye," he said, "they tell me he's missing."

"I reckon we'd better search the place," I said. "Can you rustle up any volunteers?"

"There's a barful right here, Mr Rhea," he smiled and within minutes I had thirty men on the car park, all volunteering for the hunt. I told them the situation and provided a description of the old man. As it was dark by this time, we needed lights and this caused no problem. All were local men and each could produce a torch.

I allocated teams of two men to every path and road and allowed them two hours for their search. As it was almost nine o'clock, I said we'd all meet back in the pub at eleven to compare notes. I felt sure we would secure a drink apiece, being friends of the licensee. I had a map in the car and would cross off the examined sections as they were cleared. I told Jane Jobling of our actions and she was pleased; I said that if this spontaneous search, by local men who knew the terrain, produced nothing I would call in a police search team, complete with dogs. That would take time to arrange.

We went to work as only a team of volunteers can, and I found myself paired with a youngster called John Fellows, an apprentice plumber.

"Did you know Awd Simon?" I asked John as we began our search.

"Yes," he said fondly. "He told me all about trains, Mr Rhea. I got a Hornby train when I was a lad, and he told me all about signals, engine types and so on."

"Where do you reckon he is, then?" I asked.

"We were talking in the pub before you came in," he said seriously. "Some of us reckoned he might have gone onto the line."

"The line?"

"Aye, he often went down the line, walking the sleepers like he did when he worked."

"I never thought of that!" I had to admit. "Which was his favourite part of the line?"

"Down near the beck. There's a level-crossing down there, near Marshlands Farm. He sometimes went there."

"Let's go," I said.

The walk across the muddy fields and farm tracks took us about twenty minutes and eventually we had reached the area known to the lad. The line was a single track here, running through narrow openings and thick with shrubs and trees, and there was a farm crossing. Here the line was open with no gates. This meant farmers and their workers had to be alert to the possibility of an advancing train, but to my knowledge there'd been no accidents.

"You go east, I'll go west," I said.

John obeyed. Together we gained access to the railway line and I began to walk along the sleepers, quickly acquiring the necessary pace as my feet adjusted to the regular small steps.

"Five minutes that way!" I called and John waved his torch in reply.

I walked along the line, my torch picking out the railway furniture, the glistening metals, the rows of wooden sleepers like an eternal staircase leading nowhere, while in the darkness of the vegetation tiny pinpricks of light showed. Glowworms were abroad — it was Walter de la Mare who wrote: "But dusk would come in the apple boughs, the green of the glow-worm shine. The birds in the nest would crouch to rest, and home I'd trudge to mine."

And then I found him.

Quite suddenly, quite horribly, I found Awd Simon.

He was lying between the rails, quite dead, battered and bloody. Poor, poor man. He was clad in his railway clothes, with his bait bag across his shoulder while his peaked cap lay several yards away, knocked from his head.

I stood for a full minute looking upon his battered and torn body, wondering why. Was this an accident or was it deliberate? Had he donned his workaday clothes of yesteryear for the sole purpose of undertaking his own final sentimental journey? Was it so impossible for Awd Simon to tolerate life without his beloved railways?

I shall never know.

He could have sprung from these thick bushes without the driver ever realising.

"John," I shouted to the lad, for we had to return to the village.

I had work to do.

# CHAPTER EIGHT

Even a child is known by his doings.
*Book of Proverbs*, xx 11

It was William Blake who wrote "when the voices of children are heard on the green, and laughing is heard on the hill", but I suspect that the author of that resounding phrase "Children should be seen and not heard" lived in a village. Playing children do make a terrible noise and the larger their numbers the greater the noise. In play, children display a desperate desire to shout louder than their friends and their high-spirited physical antics tend to annoy those residents whose gardens receive footballs, whose greenhouses swallow cricket-balls and whose chimney-pots fly badly routed kites.

Rural children are better off than their city and suburban cousins because they have acres of fields and lots of open space to use for the noisy release of their excess energies, but this does not encourage them to play away from home all the time. Somehow they contrive to play where nobody wants them. All children love playing near their homes or, better still, near someone else's home. While most adults will tolerate their good-natured noise and their unintentional vandalism of rose-beds and windows, there is a hard core of householders who persistently telephone the village constable to complain about playing children.

Since the beginning of constabulary duties, policemen have suffered from this incessant complaining. They have been told loudly of children sliding down icy roads, jumping on rickety roofs, torturing cats or plaguing dogs, building houses in unsafe trees, killing each other or demolishing valuable property . . .

And always, by the time the policeman arrives, the children have vanished and the misdeeds have ended. Policemen know how the system works, consequently they do not rush to the scene of a complaint in a flurry of blue lights and rising dust. Instead, they proceed at a leisurely pace, knowing full well that the subjects of the irate complaint will have scarpered into prearranged hiding-places at the first hint of trouble from long-suffering adults. By arriving at an empty scene, the police officer preserves everyone's dignity. The system operates something like this. The children have succeeded in annoying their victim, which is what they require; the victim has called in the police, who have responded, so he is happy, and the policeman is content because, knowing human nature somewhat better than most, he realises that his leisurely "action" keeps everyone sweet. There are no upset parents, no children to brag about being nicked and no reports or summonses for him to waste time in submitting. It is a very diplomatic arrangement, practised over the nation by discerning police officers. It keeps politicians happy about the incidence of juvenile crime and professional social workers happy that their skills are producing fruit.

It is true, however, that children's games can get out of hand. This is frequently the case when children discover a victim who responds violently to their taunts. The more he responds, the better the children like it, and the more he will be taunted by them. They knock on his door and run away, they smear paint on his windows or pull up his plants, they perpetrate all manner of hooligan pranks upon the unfortunate person who rises to the occasion for their entertainment.

Children like nothing better than an outraged adult threatening hell, fire and thunder from the safety of his curtilage. And another thing, no sensible adult will attempt to chase the children — this hasn't a hope in hell of achieving anything, other than a grievous loss of dignity by the adult and a repeat performance by the kids in the very near future.

It is far, far better to ignore their taunts. Children whose actions do not raise a flicker of interest from their victim rapidly lose interest. Quite often, the teasing of adults by children is a psychological battle which the youngsters win due to their instinctive understanding of human nature. Adults do not react in quite the same instinctive way and very often provide a memorable display of free entertainment.

The policeman must always bear in mind that children can get out of hand and wreak damage or injury if not checked. Old people can get hurt or shocked by youthful actions, but somewhere in the centre of this long-running conflict there is a level of tolerance which can be achieved by all parties. It is the duty of the village bobby to find that middle course.

I found myself seeking such a course in Ashfordly one autumn afternoon. It involved a formidable lady who stood almost six feet tall in her silk stockings and had a nose as long as Saltburn pier. Domineering and undoubtedly severe, she lived alone in a rambling house on the outskirts of Ashfordly and dressed characteristically in tweed skirts with pleats, brogue shoes with the tongues sticking out and hats that looked like fish-wives' bonnets. Her dark hair was severely styled with large slides holding it back above the ears and she spoke with a heavy accent which suggested a lineage of high-class breeding. She was Miss Deirdre Finlay who may have been in her mid-forties and who drove a little Morris estate car which was always full of plant pots and fertilizer sacks. She strode about the town as if she wore seven-league boots.

I do not believe she had a job of any sort. I understand she existed on a legacy from Daddy although she did grow plants of all kinds which she sold to the local greengrocers, fruiterers and market traders. Certainly this activity alone was insufficient to support her but it kept her occupied and probably brought in a few pounds cash every week, tax-free.

Her garden was one of the old-fashioned enclosed type, surrounded entirely by a tall brick wall a good eight feet high. Inside, it was suitably secluded and private and within those high walls Miss Finlay grew her widely assorted plants. One corner was devoted to apple-trees, all neatly pruned and all expert at producing a wide range of Bramley's, Cox's Orange Pippin and other soundly established varieties. She sold these too and made a useful income from her stock of sixty trees.

Late that autumn afternoon, it was fortuitous that I was patrolling the Ashfordly area. I had parked the motorcycle and was enjoying a leisurely foot patrol around the market square, admiring the shops, the pubs and the pretty women who always seemed to be going somewhere important. During those blissful perambulations, I wandered through the streets away from the town centre and found myself patrolling along Water End. This was where a small stream, which meandered from the surrounding hills, joined the river and it was a very pleasant and pretty part of the town.

Miss Finlay's house was upon the side of this beck and it was by sheer chance that she poked that formidable head around her gatepost just as I was passing.

"Constable!" she called loudly as she noticed me. "A minute, if you don't mind."

I approached her with a smile on my face. Although we had never spoken before, I knew of this lady and her fierce reputation. I decided to be pleasant to her.

"Yes?"

"You are new?"

"I am. I'm P.C. Rhea from Aidensfield. I'm patrolling the town this afternoon."

"Then I have work for you. I have caught a thief."

"A thief?" I must have sounded surprised.

"Yes, a thieving youth, a good-for-nothing layabout. He was stealing my apples."

I looked around the gatepost and into her spacious grounds but saw no captured youth.

"Where is he?"

"I have locked him in my potato store," and she suddenly grinned. "That'll teach him, what?"

"Take me to him," I suggested. I wondered what sort of thief this was.

She took me into the well-kept grounds and at the side of her beautiful home there was an array of outbuildings, one of which was resounding with loud thumps and frenzied cries of "Let me out."

"In there." She pointed to a closed door. It was of solid wood with a padlock slipped neatly through a stout hasp, securely imprisoning the villain.

"Who is it?" I called through the door before releasing him.

"I cannot say." She shook her notable head. "I have not seen him before."

The door rattled and banged as the incarcerated rogue attempted to regain his freedom, so I shouted, "It's the police."

The banging stopped and I heard a whispered voice inside say, "Oh, bloody hell."

"Who's in there?" I called through the wooden panels.

No reply.

I began to slip the padlock from the hasp, so she warned me. "He's quick, Officer, you'll have to watch him. I had trouble, you know; it's a good job I'm fit. Hockey, you know. It keeps me trim."

I smiled an unspoken answer to that claim and carefully unbolted the door. It opened easily and there, blinking in the sudden flood of daylight, was a diminutive youth with carroty hair and elfin features set in a freckled face. He made no effort to gallop to freedom, possibly because both I and Miss Finlay occupied the doorway of the potato-house and effectively prevented any exit. To this tiny lad, the opposition must have looked formidable.

"And who are you?" I put to him.

"Ian Fenwick," he said with a faint Scots accent. He didn't look into my eyes, but spent most of the interview contemplating the dusty stone floor of his cell.

"How old are you?"

"Sixteen."

"You're very small for sixteen," I said, for he looked no more than fourteen, perhaps even less.

"I'm an apprentice jockey," he said. "Jockeys are small."

"And where do you live?"

"Here, I'm with the racing stable round the back."

I knew the place. It was a successful racing stable on the outskirts of Ashfordly, positioned literally a stone's throw behind Miss Finlay's house. Some good winners had been bred here and the proprietor, a big Irishman called Brendan O'Shea, was building himself a useful reputation in this highly competitive field. He employed around a dozen stable-boys and apprentices and inevitably they found themselves in trouble from time to time. But I'd never caught one stealing apples before.

"O'Shea's place?" I asked, waiting for his confirming answer.

"You won't tell Mr O'Shea, will you?" He raised his brown eyes from the floor and looked at us both. I recognised a genuine look of sorrow on his face. This was no regular thief.

"Let's hear your story." I decided I must know a little more about this curious episode. "Miss Finlay says she caught you stealing apples. That's a crime, you know, and at your age it could mean a court appearance."

"Oh, Jesus!" He blanched. "Not that . . . not for apples . . ."

"You must admit it then?" I put to him as we contained him in the shed.

He hung his head.

"I'm sorry, it was for the horse."

"The horse?" I said. "What horse?"

165

"The one I ride most, Nature's Signal. She loves apples and there are times she won't behave unless she gets one. I didn't have one so I came over the wall. She was getting stroppy, sir . . ."

"And I was waiting," came in Miss Finlay. "Caught him red-handed, I did."

"Did you get any?" I asked the lad.

"Aye, three," he said. "She took them off me."

"It is not the first time my apples have been attacked," she countered. "It seems that some children regard my walls as a challenge, Constable . . ."

"Is this your first time?" I asked the little youth.

He nodded. "We usually have a good stock of apples for the horses, and for Nature's Signal in particular, but, well, there weren't any and she was getting stroppy . . . all I needed was four or five . . ."

"If he'd asked, would you have given him some?" I asked Miss Finlay.

"I'd have sold him a pound or two, perhaps," she said without batting an eyelid.

"You know it's wrong to steal?" I put to Fenwick, still treating him like a child in spite of his age. His diminutive stature was off-putting.

"I didn't know whose they were and it was urgent," he explained. "I'm not a thief . . ."

"I've a good mind to tell your boss!" Miss Finlay suddenly interrupted, and I wondered if she was softening a little, perhaps regretting her hasty action and hard attitude.

"Please, no. He'll sack me, I know he will. He's tough, sir, very tough with us."

"If you go to court, it will be all over the papers anyway," I pointed out, knowing I'd have to interview this youth formally in the presence of some adult if I was to take official action.

"What are you going to do with him, Constable?" I couldn't help noticing that Miss Finlay's voice had softened considerably.

"Well." I decided to put a little bit of pressure upon her. "There are several courses open to me. If you are prepared to attend court as a witness and give evidence, I will take him to the police station. His guardian will be called and charges of larceny will be preferred. He will appear at a juvenile court in due course. That's one course of action."

She swallowed, but did not commit herself to being a witness.

"The second is for me to report him for summons. You would still be required as a witness in court during the hearing, but I would not have to arrest the lad. I would simply take his name and other details, visit his guardian's home. There I would report him for the offence of larceny in the presence of Mr O'Shea."

"And what will happen to him?" she asked with genuine interest.

"Who can tell?" I shrugged my shoulders. "The maximum penalty for simple larceny is five years in prison, but in this case we would probably proceed under Section 36 of the Larceny Act 1861, which is purely a summary offence with a small fine as the penalty. If this is Ian's first offence — and it seems it was a sudden urge as he says — the court may let him off with a conditional discharge or probation."

"Is it really necessary for him to go to court?" she asked and I knew now that she was weakening greatly.

"Miss Finlay, you have arrested a thief, and you have handed that thief over to me, having accused him of a serious crime. I am duty-bound to take official action." I thought I'd let her stew awhile with those thoughts.

She licked her lips and I saw the lad's eyes turn away from us. He resumed his worried contemplation of the flagged floor.

"You just happened to be walking past . . ." she began, almost apologetically.

"There is another way of dealing with the matter," I said slowly and she regarded me quizzically.

"Tell me," and there was a note of appeal in her voice.

"If you decide not to press charges, it would be possible for me to deal with the matter here and now." I played my trump-card.

"Really? I wanted him taught a lesson, people must learn that they cannot help themselves to other's belongings . . ."

"I won't do it again, I promise . . ." cried our prisoner.

"What must I do?" she turned to me. I knew she'd abandoned the idea of a prosecution.

"You've a lot of apple-trees." I turned and regarded them.

"Sixty," she said. "All fruit-bearing as you can see."

"And you pick all that fruit yourself?"

"I pay someone, it's a long job working alone. Too long when I'm busy."

Now I turned to Ian.

"Do you like picking apples, young man?"

He didn't answer. I think he knew what was going through my mind.

"Miss Finlay, if this young man agreed to pick all your apples without payment, would you drop your charges of larceny?"

For a moment, her face did not crack, and suddenly she smiled, showing acres of large brown teeth.

"I think that's an excellent compromise, Constable. But how can I be sure he picks them?"

"If he doesn't, we will tell Mr O'Shea what he's done."

"And if he does pick them?"

"We do nothing else. We don't tell Mr O'Shea, we don't trouble the courts with this, and you will not have to take time off work to give evidence."

She looked at the shivering lad, still held in the potato-shed, and said, "Well?"

"I'll start tonight," he whispered. "I'll do it — I'll pick them all for you, honest."

"Right," I said. "That's it. The problem is solved."

I told the lad to leave us immediately and when he had galloped out of sight I said, "Make sure he does it, Miss

Finlay. Make him pick all your apples. If he doesn't, you must come back to me and I'll speak to Mr O'Shea."

"I like your idea, Constable. To be truthful, I couldn't bear the thought of him going to court . . ."

I couldn't tell her that I didn't relish the idea of prosecuting the lad for stealing apples; what the inspector would have thought if I had, I daren't even consider. I left her garden feeling confident that Ian Fenwick would return to begin the long chore of picking stones of apples.

A fortnight later, I was in Ashfordly again and decided to check with Miss Finlay, just to ensure the deal had been carried out. She was delighted to see me, so much so that she invited me in for a coffee. As I sat at her scrubbed table in the rustic kitchen, she produced a hot coffee in a large mug.

"Mr Rhea, isn't it?" she asked, as if reminding herself of my name.

"Yes," I confirmed.

"Mr Rhea, that apple-picking idea was marvellous. That young man has carefully picked all my apples, and in fact comes round to work in his spare time. I pay him, of course, for this extra work. He's excellent, and a real nice young man. And that horse — she's a beauty, a real temperamental filly, and he knows just how to handle her . . . I give him apples, for the horse, you know . . . and he has tea with me sometimes . . ."

And as she prattled on I could see the light of lost motherhood in her eyes. Miss Finlay had become a very happy woman.

* * *

One eternal problem for the police officer is the gang of youths who persist in misbehaving. Such gangs are found everywhere, in all nations and in large cities or small towns. They are often male-dominated although girls are known to join them and indeed the so-called gentle sex can prove formidable leaders.

Even villages produce gangs of youngsters and the effect upon the neighbourhood is the same as that produced by their larger and more violent counterparts in the city. They worry the public. Policemen know that these gangs are inevitable; every year new gangs form as the older ones decline and, in the urban areas, they often call themselves by distinctive names as they compete for power against others of similar background. Such competition is rare in the small villages of North Yorkshire; occasionally, a rival mob from a market town will descend upon a dance in a peaceful village and wreak havoc among the local youths but juvenile demonstrations of this kind of strength are seldom a real threat to the peace and tranquillity of a community. They are little more than a temporary nuisance.

Aidensfield had its own gang. I could see it blossoming as the warmer nights took control. Several youths began to congregate around the memorial seat beside the telephone kiosk and this became their meeting-place. Each evening around six-thirty, six or seven of them would gather, some with motorcycles and others without. Several of them showed their masculinity by smoking and laughing loudly as the citizens passed by, and the gathering was little more than a typical youthful show of collective strength. On their own, these lads were fine, but when placed within a gang they could be led into all kinds of situations, chiefly those of mischief and trouble.

From the policeman's viewpoint, these gangs are an interesting phenomenon. Every year, the pattern repeats itself — youths gather, dress alike, act alike, make a lot of noise, ogle girls and upset older folks. They make noise and laughter, leave litter and beer-cans around and within two years disappear as their maturing members make their way in the greater world. Then another gang takes its place; younger youths begin all over again and the pattern is repeated . . .

Head-shrinkers and clever people attempt to find reasons for such assemblies, but I'm sure it is a natural phenomenon among the youths; they meet their own kind for social reasons; they show off, brag about their strength and powers, challenge adults and the law, and generally let off steam. If vandalism creeps in, then it is part of the charade of youth and never a serious threat to society, albeit, very annoying at the time.

It is part and parcel of a police officer's duty to deal with such gangs and it can be a shade daunting for a young officer to confront a fierce and threatening gathering of youths in order to curtail their more effusive outflowings. As a young bobby, before coming to Aidensfield, I had had my share of such gatherings and somehow managed to escape unscathed. In those days, people did not physically attack policemen and the gangs of youths nurtured a grudging respect for the policeman who moved them along or who compelled them to pick up their waste chip papers or empty bottles.

My early days of coping with rebellious urban youths was excellent training for the time I might have to cope with similar problems at Aidensfield. Sure enough, the occasion did arise.

I had watched the growth of the Aidensfield gang soon after my arrival. The summer nights brought them out and these teenage lads began to assemble near the memorial seat, as generations of previous lads had done. They did nothing alarming, although one or two elder folk did express concern. This was inevitable — a collection of high-spirited lads in outrageous clothes kicking a football about the road or chasing empty beer-cans to the accompaniment of loud shouts and curses was a little disconcerting, albeit harmless.

Their ages would be from fifteen to seventeen or eighteen, chiefly schoolchildren or sometimes those unable or unwilling to find work. Boredom brought them together and bravado compelled them to elect a member to visit the pub in an attempt to buy cider or beer. The landlord knew them and refused, so they drank lemonade or bottled shandy.

The problem was what to do with them. If they were not checked, their boisterous fun could lead to trouble. From a policeman's point of view, his duty is to maintain law and

order and when assemblies of big lads begin to cause alarm he must do something about it. Inevitably, there are complaints from the residents if the situation gets out of hand, and occasionally the parish council sounds off by writing to the Press or to the Chief Constable. But what can a policeman do against a pack of cunning lads who behave when he's there and who promptly retaliate the moment his back is turned?

Some police officers have started youth clubs, others have created sporting clubs for football or cricket and all kinds of youth organisations have grown in an attempt to keep bored teenagers off the streets and away from situations of conflict with society. Such schemes had been running in and near Aidensfield for some time. There was a very good youth club in Ashfordly, a billiards club in Maddleskirk, several football and cricket teams, and still the lads congregated in villages with noisy bikes and foul language.

I had words with them; I even threatened to take them to court and for a time peace reigned. But the moment I was away the villagers began to complain. The lads were playing football in the street, upsetting motorists and kicking balls into gardens. Beer-bottles and waste paper were left around or smashed on the footpaths, old folks were jeered and vandalism began to materialise. On two occasions, car aerials were broken and windows smashed . . .

This was now serious. I decided to take a hard look at the members of this troublesome set-up. Most of them were ordinary decent lads, somehow caught up in the relentless pressure put on them by more senior and more forceful characters. Each time I patrolled Aidensfield, I noted the names of the lads gathered in the village street, sometimes stopping to talk with them and sometimes merely passing by. If I became too strict with them and too niggardly about their behaviour, they would react against me and cause even more trouble when my back was turned. So I had to find another way. And my earlier days at Strensford helped.

There was one youth in the Aidensfield gang who was clearly the leader. Every gang has its leader and this was a

dark-haired youth of striking good looks but whose person-
ality was defective in some way. He was always at the centre
of trouble, I noted, always making a noise, always shouting
the loudest. I learned that his name was Alan Maskell.

I wanted to learn more about the lad. Over the next few
days, I learned he lived in a council house, that his father
had run off with a bus-conductress from York and that his
mother spent her money and her time in the pub. Alan had
gone to the local secondary school and had achieved moderate success in spite of his background, but at the age of
sixteen there seemed no real future for him. He had no desire
to leave the village and no real chance of a worthwhile job
here. He could become a labourer on a building site, or a
washer-up in a local hotel, but little more. It wasn't a bright
future and his rebellion could be understood.

Tall and good-looking, he was a powerful lad. His active
eyes told me he had a natural intelligence, if no great aca-
demic qualities. I could imagine him displaying a manual
skill of some kind — bricklaying perhaps, or metal-work of
some sort. When I talked to him man to man, alone and
without his audience of adoring youngsters, he was fine. I
liked him and in some ways felt sorry that his family background had let him down. With help and encouragement,
this youth could do well. But who was to spend the necessary
time and energy sorting him out?

I learned he was fond of animals and that he bred white
rabbits; alone at home as a younger child, he had spent his
spare time with his rabbits and now had a very good collection. At home, with his rabbits, he was a totally different
character. Gentle and loving towards them, he worshipped
the creatures and it was difficult to link this gentle lad with
the toughie who ruled the others in the village street.

During that summer, I had repeated complaints about
the conduct of the lads, and indeed the gathering was growing. Others from afar came to join them and I knew that if
I wasn't careful I'd have serious trouble on my hands. The
matter came to a head late one August evening.

I was on duty in Ashfordly and was unaware that some two dozen lads had congregated in Aidensfield, many with motorcycles. They had started to race up and down the street and this bit of fun had developed into a noisy and dangerous battle. Cheering, drinking and shouting abuse at the villagers had developed and the incoming bunch had virtually taken over. The local lads were jealous of their hard-man image too and so a battle of pride developed.

I received a telephone call about it; someone in the village had telephoned Mary who managed to trace me in Ashfordly and I drove in the section car to my own village. When I arrived, Alan was still there with the local lads, and one or two outsiders remaining, chortling at my presence.

My first job was to check all driving licences and insurance for their motorcycles, and then to check the machines themselves for noisy exhausts and other legal defects. Next, I warned the motorcyclists about the illegality of dangerous driving, careless driving and racing on the highway, and threatened court action against anyone found in the future doing any of those actions. And a court appearance could lead eventually to disqualification of their hard-won driving licences. I made a list of all their names and addresses, motorcycle registration numbers and their own appearances. I then told them I would circulate those details to all my colleagues in the district — any more motorcycle problems would result in heavy penalties against the offenders.

Next, I turned to the local lads without motorcycles. They had been carried away by the excitement of the situation and continued to laugh and swagger about in group bravado as I lectured on their behaviour. Finally I turned to Alan Maskell.

"Alan," I said loudly, "I've a special message for you."

Before his adoring audience, he swaggered over to me, chewing something and winking at his friends.

"Yeh?"

"I'm putting you in charge of these lads," I said.

"Me?"

"Yes, you."

"In charge of them?" The swagger had gone already.

"Yes, in charge of them." I had to get the message firmly home, and they all listened.

He looked about them all and grinned. "Hey, you lot. I'm the boss."

"Yes, Alan, and that means you are responsible for their behaviour. If anything happens in this village — broken windows, litter, complaints about trouble, vandalism — then you will go to court. You, Alan. I'm making you responsible for the conduct of this lot. If they behave, you don't go to court. If they misbehave, you will have to answer in court for them. Do you understand?"

There was silence as Alan and the others began to comprehend the magnitude of the situation.

"You mean if he puts a window through, you'll have me, Mr Rhea?"

"Yes, Alan, that's what I mean. I've had enough of you and this lot. People are always complaining, and I've got to leave more important things to come down here, like tonight, and give you a bulling. So, as from today, you're the boss. It's your job to keep them straight. I'm going to pass the word around my colleagues and, if there's any more trouble in Aidensfield, they'll come looking for you."

"Bloody hell, Mr Rhea, you can't do that . . ."

"I've just done it, Alan. It starts now. I mean it — every word."

"I could be fined or sent away?"

"You could, so you'll have to sort them out, eh?"

I could see the lad was shaken by his responsibility. Whether it would work, I didn't know. Alan was certainly the ring-leader, but whether the others would obey him when he called for *good* behaviour was a different matter. I knew some of the younger element worshipped him and I felt they would behave out of respect or admiration for him, not wishing him to suffer on their behalf.

As I stood my ground, the crowd of youths began to disintegrate. The motorcyclists drove away, not revving and roaring out of the village as was their normal practice, but driving sedately through the houses. Next time they came, I would check their documents and vehicles again . . . and so would my colleagues. We'd soon sicken unwelcome troublemakers.

Alan and his crowd of locals drifted away too, wandering towards their homes as I remained near the seat.

The next night, no one turned up at the seat. I walked around Aidensfield seeking them and wondered where they'd gone. Eventually I found them on the cricket field. They were playing a practice game and Alan was organising them into two teams. He saw me and came across.

"I asked the cricket captain for permission, Mr Rhea, and he said . . ."

"Fine, Alan, you're doing a good job. Why not challenge the village team to a game one day? When your lads are practised up, eh?"

His eyes lit up. "Aye," he said. "Aye, I'll do that."

Alan and his pals caused me no further trouble. They did congregate near the telephone kiosk from time to time, and they did ride their motorbikes around the place, but always in a reasonable manner. Later that year, Alan joined the Army and was subsequently posted to Germany. His gang caused me no further trouble because they had grown up.

Next year, another set of noisy lads would take their place and that meant I'd have to find someone else to take charge.

I would start my search immediately.

\* \* \*

Another problem child was young Stephen Matthews. He was six years old with a round, cheeky face and mischievous blue eyes. His hair was sandy in colour and his fit little body spent its time galloping everywhere noisily in the sheer exuberance of youth. He was not a criminal; even if his activities had been of the kind that could be classed as criminal, he would not have been prosecuted due to his tender age. His problem was simple — he kept getting lost.

Stephen had a propensity for running away. If his beleaguered mother took him shopping in York or Ashfordly, it could be guaranteed that Stephen would lose her. The poor woman must have spent hours seeking him and the police officers in the area knew Stephen by name and description. His longest period of absence was one full day; on that occasion, he went with a school outing to Scarborough and promptly got lost among the trippers. His mother was there to supervise him, but he managed to give her the slip; she knew him well enough to remain where she was, and that he'd return eventually. But on that occasion he did not, for he spent the afternoon sitting in the police station until mother arrived distraught and anxious.

At home in Aidensfield, his disappearances were monotonously regular. He would vanish on the way home from school, or from the pack of cubs he had joined; he wandered off into the woods and fields, looking for rabbits or birds, seeking excitement in nature. Time and time again, Mrs Matthews called me to help in searching for the little lad, and time and time again we found him wandering the lanes blissfully unaware of the panic about him. No amount of tellings-off and advice seemed to penetrate his mind, for Stephen would always get lost. I felt sorry for his parents and wondered what his maturity would be like. I could see his wife would have problems.

It was natural that I rapidly grew acquainted with both the little lad and his parents. I developed the practice, whenever I saw Stephen alone, of asking him where he was going, whom he was going to see and whether his mother knew where he was. This oft-repeated dialogue gradually resulted in Stephen's telling me the answers before I asked the questions, and if he saw me in the village he would say, "Mr Rhea, I'm going to see my Aunt Phyllis and Mummy knows about it." or "Mummy sent me to the shop, Mr Rhea, for some tea and bread. I'm going home now and won't be late . . ."

He was a marvellously confident little chap, and most likeable, but in the summer he performed yet another of his vanishing tricks. Mrs Matthews telephoned to ask if I'd seen Stephen because he had not come in from school. I had to say I had not seen him. As things were, I was about to walk down the village to talk to a farmer about a movement licence for his pigs, so I promised Mrs Matthews I'd keep an eye open for her errant child.

As I entered Norman Berriman's farmyard, the very first person I saw leaving was young Stephen. He had a pup with him.

"Now, young man." I adopted a stern attitude. "I've had your mum ringing me about you. You didn't go home from school and she's worried . . ."

"I'm going now, Mr Rhea. I just called in to see Mr Berriman about this puppy, you see . . ."

And off he went. I watched the pair of them walk along the village street, the lad towing the disinterested pup with a long piece of string until they turned down the road towards Stephen's home. I thought no more of the incident until I had concluded my business with Farmer Berriman and happened to mention Stephen's name.

"Aye," said Berriman. "Yon little chap came in and asked if he could have a pup."

"I wonder if his mother knows?" I said, almost to myself.

"Now, that's summat I don't know," the farmer said. "He told me his mam did know and said it was all right. I gave him yon dog — it's a mongrel dog pup, and grand little animal. I can't do with more dogs than I've got and was pleased to give it a home . . ."

"Has Stephen been here before?" I asked.

"Aye, more than once. He oft comes in after school, checking the dogs and seeing to the cows. Canny little lad, isn't he?"

"He drives his mother up the wall," I laughed. "She never knows where he gets to . . ."

"He seldom stays long," smiled Norman Berriman. "Comes in here, feeds the hens mebbe or watches me milking sometimes, then off he goes, running down the street. Always at a gallop, isn't he?"

As I talked, I got the distinct feeling that Mrs Matthews would know nothing of the acquisition of that pup. Knowing of Stephen's cunning, he would have chatted to Mr Berriman until the farmer had given him the dog. But it was no problem of mine. It was something the Matthews family would have to sort out with the farmer. However, when I returned home, I rang Mrs Matthews to inform her that I had seen Stephen and that he was heading for home.

"Yes," she said gently on the telephone. "He arrived home safe and sound, Mr Rhea — and he had a pup with him. He said the farmer gave it to him."

"He did, I talked with Mr Berriman about it."

"I knew nothing of that, Mr Rhea. The young monkey's gone and got himself a dog without our permission, and now he won't part with it . . ."

"It might keep him at home," I said wryly. "If he has to feed his dog and exercise it, he might come straight home from school."

"But we don't want a dog, Mr Rhea. I don't know what my husband will say when he comes home."

"I'm sure Mr Berriman will take it back when he knows the truth. He thought you knew all about it."

"I'll have words with him. Thank you, Mr Rhea."

I have no idea what transpired between father and son, father and mother, or mother and son, but the outcome was that Stephen kept the dog. Thereafter, I often saw them together, with Stephen eternally running and the growing dog galloping at his side. Sometimes the dog was on a lead and sometimes it ran free beside its young master. They were a happy sight.

Although the dog was a mongrel, it had the appearance of a black and white cur, typical of the sheep-dogs in this area. It was a pleasant and lovable animal and Stephen named it Skip. Over the weeks, the pair became inseparable. Where one went, the other followed. I never spoke to Stephen's father about the animal as I seldom saw him, although Mrs

Matthews did chat with me from time to time as she went about the village. I learned that the unexpected acquisition had caused a lot of friction in the home, especially from Stephen's dad, who disliked animals at the best of times. But the lad's pleas and his mother's backing had beaten Dad, and the dog became part of the family.

The other bonus was just as I had anticipated — Stephen did not get lost quite so often, especially on his journeys home from school. He always galloped home to take Skip for a walk, although he was sometimes late from these expeditions. Mrs Matthews rang me less and less, for now she had a growing boy and a growing dog to get lost, but between them the wandering couple always returned home.

I wondered if the dog was responsible for taking Stephen home. A hungry dog will find its way to a known food supply and as the dark nights of autumn approached I received fewer calls about Stephen's disappearances.

But when I was next asked to help it was a very serious matter indeed. I don't think anyone realised at the time just how worried I had become.

I was on duty late on Friday evening because the Slemmington Hunt was holding its annual Ball in Aidensfield Village Hall. This was one of the highlights of the year. The Ball was always held on the first Friday in December in Aidensfield's beautiful village hall. This spacious building has a sprung floor which makes it ideal for ballroom dancing, and there is also a balcony, lots of anterooms and space for a bar, and although it is a somewhat remote village it has been host to many important functions. I had to be on duty in case of public order problems and at nine o'clock began to patrol the village on foot. It was bitterly cold, with a hard frost and a forecast of snow before dawn. I was well wrapped up and it would be around 9.30 that evening when Stephen's father, Desmond Matthews, hailed me outside the dance hall.

"Mr Rhea," he said and in the light of the doorway I could see the worried expression on his face. "It's Stephen again."

"Another absence?" I asked.

He nodded. "He went out about seven o'clock and hasn't come back. It's dark, you see, and he never stays out in the dark . . . I've searched everywhere, and my wife too. He's taken a torch and just vanished — and the dog with him."

"Did he give any idea where he was going?" I asked, and a fleeting thought crossed my mind that it was unusual for Mr Matthews to come to me. On every previous occasion, his wife had set the ball rolling.

"No, nothing," was all the man said.

I could sense the concern in his voice and instinctively knew I had a major problem on my hands. A search for a child at any time is harrowing, but on a bitterly cold December night it has much more relevance and urgency. Cold can be a vicious killer.

The problem was where to begin and who should conduct the search. Could one father and one policeman adequately search the wild and expansive acres of this area in the dark? Even if we had some clue as to his whereabouts, it would not be easy, but with no idea of his probable location it seemed impossible. The sheer size of the area and the time element combined to produce immense problems.

"Wait here, Mr Matthews, I'll ring Sergeant Blaketon at Ashfordly to see if we can get reinforcements."

I went to the Brewers Arms next door to the village hall and asked if I could use the telephone. Consent was immediate and I rang my section office. There was no reply. I next decided to ring the Sub-Division and managed to raise a constable on the enquiry desk.

"It's Nick," I announced. "Have you any idea where Sergeant Blaketon is, Harry?"

"He booked off the air at Eltering about half an hour ago," Harry told me. "Shall I ring him?"

"Please. I've got a missing child at Aidensfield — I'll begin the hunt now, and will return to the village hall on the hour. I reckon we might need help."

"What about police dogs? Delta Four-Seven is on the air with two dogs. I can send them over if you like."

"Yes, fine. When can they be here?"

"Twenty minutes I reckon. Can you wait?"

"I'll make a point of waiting. Can they meet me outside the village hall at Aidensfield?"

"I'll fix that, Nick. And I'll get Sergeant Blaketon to rendezvous with you as well. I take it you'll need volunteers?"

"I'm sure I will, but I think we'd better make a preliminary search of the village. I don't want to drag everybody out if he's lying asleep in a local barn. I'll ring you back if I need more help."

Now that the official wheels had started to turn, I told Mr Matthews what I'd done. I asked him to return home to make a further thorough search of the house and its surrounds, and also Stephen's known haunts. I said I'd do a quick recce of the village territory, including Norman Berriman's farm buildings and other likely places. There were the school grounds, the cricket pavilion, the churchyard, the river-banks and so forth.

I couldn't ignore my other responsibility and already, the dance was beginning to warm up. Dinner-jacketed men and ladies in flowing gowns were arriving thick and fast, so I entered the hall and found the organiser, Colonel B. J. Smithson. I told him of the development and asked him to excuse my absence, saying I'd return as soon as possible.

"Not a bit, old boy, good hunting." He dismissed me with a wave of his elegant hand.

I spent a hectic half hour searching the village and calling Stephen's name, all to no avail. I returned to the village hall and found the police dogs had arrived with two handlers. I decided we should visit Stephen's home first, to see if the parents had any further news.

Mrs Matthews was at home, waiting in case the absent pair returned, and Mr Matthews was out with a neighbour, searching some nearby woodland.

"I've got two police dogs, Mrs Matthews," I said. "We're just deciding where to deploy them."

"Will they hear Skip bark, Mr Rhea?" she asked.

"They might make him bark. Now, what time did Stephen set off?"

The dog-handlers and I listened to her story and we learned he'd eaten his tea about half past five and had then watched television for a while. At seven he had left the house and hadn't been seen since. We obtained a description of the clothes he wore, together with the dog's particulars, and I decided it was time to circulate them to all our mobiles and fixed stations. Some patrolling police officer might see them on the road somewhere. A lorry could have picked them up — anything could have happened.

I was not satisfied about the reason for Stephen's departure. Mrs Matthews did not give a reason and I found it odd that a child of six would suddenly take his dog away from the house in the dark. I wanted to know why he had left the house.

I began to probe and she broke down in tears; it seemed her husband had lost his temper with the dog because it kept scratching the paintwork of his newly painted front door and he'd threatened to shoot the bloody animal if it persisted . . .

Stephen had cried for a long time about this and at seven o'clock he'd slipped out of the house with Skip. At the time, mother was washing the pots and Dad was attending to something in the garden shed.

This news made the search even more important. On a cold December night, a child could perish from hypothermia if left out in the open, and I recognised the urgency of our actions. There was no time to lose, but where should I begin?

As I knew the village terrain very well, I suggested areas of immediate search by each of the two dogs, while I continued to examine the open buildings about Aidensfield. At eleven o'clock, Sergeant Blaketon materialised with five more officers, having been told of our lack of progress by the dog-handlers over their radios. By now, the matter was growing desperate. Stephen and his dog had been missing four hours with no indication of their whereabouts.

We asked questions around the village, but no one had seen the lad and his dog. Darkness and the fact that many villagers had been indoors preparing for the dance meant they had managed to wander off without being noticed.

With Sergeant Blaketon now in charge, the hunt assumed new proportions and I was pleased to have the vital assistance of my colleagues from the Sub-Division. I secured a map of Aidensfield and district and we apportioned a given area to each police searcher, with me providing local information about the dangers of deep waters in the streams, dangerous and ruined buildings, likely woodland hiding-places, little known routes and so forth.

Through our police radios, we were able to keep closely in touch with each other and by eleven-thirty the inspector arrived, having been told of the unsuccessful search. Now Aidensfield was alive with police vehicles, dogs and vans; men with powerful torches and loud-hailers patrolled the outer areas, all searching to a pattern and all desperately anxious to find the little fellow before the awful chill of winter took its inevitable toll.

Inside the dance hall, the huntsmen and their followers were unaware of the drama being played nearby. At half past midnight, I decided to tell Colonel Smithson of the importance of our search and to apologise for my continued absence from his function.

I found him doing a waltz with a titled lady from an adjoining hunt and I waited until he drifted past in a cloud of her expensive perfume.

"Colonel, could I speak with you?"

"Ah, Mr Rhea, of course. Found that child, have you?"

"No, we haven't," I said. "I'm just explaining my absence from your function . . ."

"What child is this?" asked her ladyship, with deep interest.

I told them both of the extent of our search and of the desperation now setting in. Her ladyship asked some very sensible questions about our methods of searching and the numbers involved, and Colonel Smithson did likewise. Their interest was intense.

"You know," he coughed, "here we are, all enjoying ourselves and that poor child is out there, on a bloody cold night . . . Mr Rhea, let us help."

"That's most generous of you," I began . . .

"Generous be damned! It's a public duty! Look — all these people know this district like the backs of their pampered hands! They've all hunted over these fields and rivers, every inch of them . . . I'll stop this bloody dance for you and ask for volunteers . . . how's that?"

"Excellent idea, Benji," beamed his lady companion. "Yes, let's join your hunt, Constable."

I was somewhat taken aback by this response but before I knew what was happening the colonel had stopped the orchestra and was addressing the assembly through the microphone. He told of the little boy's absence and of the hunt now in progress, then asked me to detail precisely what the police were doing. I took the microphone from him and gave the whole story of the missing boy and his dog. I provided a brief description of young Stephen and the clothes he was wearing, and informed the gathering that the inspector's official car, parked on the garage forecourt higher up the village, was the focal point. He had radio contact with all searchers and with Force Control at Headquarters, so this made his car the ideal Command Vehicle.

The colonel took over again.

"Right, gentlemen," he spoke into the microphone. "I think this is an occasion for us to volunteer to join the search. Everyone here knows this countryside intimately, and I'm sure the police would be grateful for any assistance. Have I any volunteers to report to the inspector's car and be allocated an area to cover?"

In the moment of silence that followed, I thought no one was going to raise a hand, but as if on an unspoken command a sea of hands was raised and he beamed with obvious delight.

"Right, that's it. Go home and change into something more useful for tramping across the landscape. And, P.C.

Rhea, if we don't find the lad tonight, we will continue tomorrow on horseback . . ."

What followed next was truly amazing. Well over half the dancers reported to the inspector's car in their evening-dress, ladies in their long flowing gowns and fur coats, and gentlemen in dinner-jackets with Wellingtons drawn from their car boots. The colonel took charge of his contingent and I could see he was thoroughly enjoying himself being back in the field of action. Others had gone home to change into more suitable attire.

By one o'clock that morning, we had well over two hundred people searching for Stephen and his dog. We allocated one policeman to each party of hunters because it meant we could maintain radio contact with our base, should the lad be discovered. I was with a party of young huntsmen and their girls from the York area, and we combed the district bordering the parish boundaries between Aidensfield and Maddleskirk. That comprised some rough landscape, thick with thorn-bushes and laced with dangerous marshland, all interspaced with deep streams and expansive open fields. We combed the area intensively by torchlight, thrashing bushes with sticks, calling the names of both boy and dog and examining every possible hiding-place. We found nothing. Even in spite of our activity, the cold was striking through our clothing.

I knew from the response on my personal radio set that the others were experiencing the same result. Nothing. There was not a clue; no sightings, nothing. It was as if the child and his dog had been spirited away.

Meticulous attention was paid to the stream which ran along the valley floor. It meandered gracefully through the fields and woods, sometimes spilling over the edge to form dangerous marshes and pools which were traps for the unwary. One team, plus a police dog, were given the specific task of searching the entire length of that stream for three miles each way. They found nothing.

Heart-warming response came from the caterers who had been booked to feed the dancers. Mr Humphries, the proprietor of the catering firm in question, had dashed home in his van to return to the scene with hot soup and sausage rolls. Although the search was of a most serious nature, it was gratifying to see the *esprit de corps* that was generated by these willing people. It was evident they were enjoying themselves, although carrying out their task with a high degree of professionalism.

None of us went to bed that night. The bitter chill gave way to an even colder dawn and as daylight broke we were a tired and bedraggled sight. Those who had not gone home to change looked a sorry mess, suits mud-spattered and torn, long elegant dresses stained and ripped and the people red-eyed and weary. We had been searching for twelve hours without a break.

At nine o'clock that morning, the inspector had to make a vital decision. His men needed rest. They needed sleep, refreshment and warmth if they were to continue; without that, there could be further casualties among the searchers. He knew the risks and I saw him look at his watch.

He called me in for a conference and we sat in his car.

"Nine o'clock, Nick. And not a bloody sausage."

"These people have been marvellous, sir," I said. "They said they would go home and get horses at dawn, if he hadn't been found."

"They're incredible. And our lads too — they've tramped miles tonight in appalling weather . . ."

"Where is everyone now, sir?" I asked.

"Still out there. Have you seen the parents?"

"The father's out somewhere and Mrs Matthews is still at home, standing by the window. I saw her as I came in."

"Let's give it another couple of hours, Nick. Can you stand it?"

"Sure," I said. "Thank God for Jack Humphries and his grub!"

I returned to my little party and left the inspector to relay his decision to the troops. We moved our group another half mile to the west and began yet another systematic search of the scrubland upon the foothills which rose towards the grim moors behind. It was tiring in the extreme.

And then, at half past nine, came some marvellous news. Stephen had been found and he was still alive — and so was the dog.

I was thrilled to hear the cheers rising from the hunters spread all over the countryside as the news was passed over the police loud-hailers and radio sets. We were all asked to return to base. It was all over.

By the time I returned, Stephen had been whisked off to hospital in one of the cars belonging to a huntsman, and his dog had been taken home. As everyone gathered around the inspector's car, he decided to thank everyone there and then, and explained how the discovery had occurred.

Miss Gabrielle Gladstone, a member of the Slemmington Hunt, had gone home to get her horse at dawn, and had decided to ride back to the Control Point via the fields. Her home was in Ploatby, several miles by road but a short ride across the fields. She was a pretty young woman of about twenty-five and as she had ridden through the fields in daylight she had recalled some of her own childhood adventures. There was a derelict mill deep in a wood, well off the beaten track, and she had decided to examine that during her trip.

And there was the boy. He had somehow found his way into that awful place in the darkness, lost his torch and fallen. He had broken an ankle, she said, and had been unable to move. He had lain all night on a pile of sacks and the fact he was indoors helped him survive. But, she said, he owed his life to his dog. It had remained with him all the time and, when she found them, the boy was curled up asleep with his arms around his faithful friend. The dog had kept the boy's body temperature sufficiently high for him to survive.

Afterwards, Mr Matthews praised the dog, he praised the hunt and he praised the police. He was overwhelmed and overjoyed at the response by the public of Aidensfield and their friends.

I never knew how the youngster had managed to find that remote place at night and I don't think he knew himself. It was so far off the beaten track that it might have escaped our attention, and I found myself wondering whether we'd have found the lad if he'd chosen to run away on a night when there was no Hunt Ball.

That Hunt Ball was a success in many ways and, thereafter, young Stephen didn't wander very far. I do know that later in the year he was a guest of honour of the hunt, who took him around the kennels to see the puppies and the foxhounds. In fact, he was presented with a whip by the Master of Foxhounds, but with strict instructions never to use it on his own dog!

# CHAPTER NINE

All happy families resemble each other,
each unhappy family is unhappy in its own way.
LEO TOLSTOY, 1828—1910

There is no doubt that families of children can lead to friendships and understanding between their respective parents and in a village community many lasting relationships have developed because parents met at school events. When our three children were too young to attend primary school, we sent them to play-school. The eldest, Elizabeth, started by going once a week. There she met and played with other youngsters and this developed her ability to mix with those of her own age before attending school. We felt it an important part of her development and it helped at primary school.

Two of her little pals were Paul and Sarah Parker, instantly recognisable as twins. Mrs Parker was then a frail slip of a girl and she lived with her twins in a council house at Maddleskirk. Her no-good husband had left her when she was nineteen, having presented her with these bairns at a very tender age. They had now reached school age and started the primary school with my Elizabeth.

Julia Parker had to be admired. Somehow she managed to earn a few pounds each week and, although she depended heavily upon the State to maintain herself and her family, she did her best to keep her youngsters well-fed and neatly clothed. Both Mary and I had a deep sympathy for her in her plight; alone, she had to support those youngsters, run the house, pay her bills and somehow retain her sanity. I do not think her awful husband ever paid a penny towards their keep in spite of repeated court orders. Certainly, he never came near the village.

Julia herself was thin and wiry; she looked eternally underfed and hungry, although she was a pretty girl with delightful eyes and a lovely face. She was never heard to complain about the plight in which she found herself, and there is no doubt that the entire village liked her. Even her twins were nice — they were pleasantly mannered kiddies and seemed able to mix well with others of their age. She had every right to be proud of them as they came towards their sixth birthday.

It was with some horror, therefore, that I received a telephone call from York Police one Saturday afternoon to ask if I knew a woman called Mrs Julia Parker of Maddleskirk.

"Yes," I said to the unknown constable at the other end. "I know Julia Parker."

"Describe her, can you?"

I did my best, emphasising her dark hair, her slenderness and her general appearance. I put her age at about twenty-three. I followed this with, "Why are you asking?"

"We've a young woman in the nick," he said. "She says her name is Julia Parker from Maddleskirk, but can't prove her identity. She named you as somebody who can identify her."

"Does my description fit the girl you've got there?"

"It does," he said. "Thanks."

"What's the matter with her?" I asked.

"She's been nicked for shoplifting," he said flatly. "She's pinched some kids' toys from a shop in town."

I groaned. "Are you sure?"

"Positive," he said. "The manager caught her and she's admitted taking the things. We're going through the necessary procedures right now — she'll be at court next Tuesday."

"You'll be bailing her?" I put to him.

"I see no problem, she says she has twins with a baby-sitter in your village."

"Yes, it'll be Mrs Hird," I guessed.

"That's the name she gave. She seems a nice kid," he added.

"She is," I said and then gave him a genuine account of Julia's family circumstances and the problems she had surmounted. He expressed sorrow but we both knew the law must take its course. I asked the constable to pass a message to Julia, asking her to pop in to see myself and Mary when she returned. She had to know she had friends.

That evening, a tearful Julia knocked at my door and we admitted her. Mary took her into the lounge where our three children were being entertained before bed and, once inside the house, she burst into tears.

"I'm so embarrassed," she began . . .

Mary made a marvellous job of comforting the girl. As the tale poured from her, we learned it was the twins' birthday next Wednesday. They would be six years old and she'd had no money to buy them anything; everything had gone on food and clothes and, in a last desperate act, she'd tried to steal a couple of toys. Other children got toys for their birthdays, she said, but hers wouldn't on this occasion . . .

It was a very sad case, and so out of character. I knew there was no answer to it — she had stolen the toys, worth about £1 each, and had admitted it. I knew she would go to court and be fined a small amount; the magistrates might, however, decide upon a conditional discharge. Whatever happened, though, it meant Julia would be dragged through the courts and her name bandied about as a common thief. We did our best to comfort her and Mary said we would try to find some toys for the children before Wednesday. At least, they'd be happy.

Julia remained with us as our youngsters were taken upstairs and we all settled down for a coffee, all the time trying to find some way of helping Julia to accept her fate and to take a positive grip on her future. She had done so well up to date, but this one slip threatened to destroy all her past efforts. She had cracked under intolerable strains and would need help and guidance over the coming weeks. Mary took it upon herself to help this slip of a girl. Eventually, she left us with a smile, and I felt happier about her. She appeared to be calm in the face of her coming ordeal.

That all occurred on the Saturday evening and, on Monday night, my telephone rang. It was the same constable from York and he told me his name was Geoff Lewis.

"It's about that girl, she's due at court tomorrow," he said. "I would like you to make sure she comes, Mr Rhea."

"We've already talked to her," I told him. "I'm on day off and my wife has some shopping to do, so we'll fetch her through. She'll be there, you can rest assured on that."

"That's good of you. Could you fetch her into the police office first? The inspector wants a word with her."

This was unusual, but I agreed.

On the Tuesday morning, we stopped the car outside Julia's tidy home and she ran to join us, having arranged for the children to visit a neighbour if she was late. No one knew of her secret and I hoped the newspapers wouldn't make too much of a fuss about it. Although she was tearful, she seemed to be in control of herself as I told her about the message from York Police. I parked at the police station, close to the River Ouse, and escorted Julia inside. I asked for P.C. Lewis and he appeared, smiling when he saw me. I guessed it was with relief at her presence.

He recognised Julia and said, "Can you come upstairs to the inspector's office?"

She looked at me and I said, "I'll come with you if you like," and turned to the policeman for his approval. He nodded. Mary and I followed them up the steep, winding staircase.

P.C. Lewis introduced me to the inspector and explained my presence; I told him of our links with Julia. He looked at me and smiled his understanding.

"Sit down, all of you," he invited.

"Julia," he addressed the worried girl. "We have been doing a bit of research into your background, and we now know that what you told us on Saturday is true. P.C. Lewis has spoken to P.C. Rhea about you."

Julia merely nodded and I've no doubt she regarded this as just another portion of routine court procedure. I didn't, but I had no idea what was happening.

"Julia," continued the inspector, "we have spoken to the manager of the shop about you. He has decided not to prefer charges — if he fails to give evidence, we cannot proceed. He will not come to court."

Tears came into her eyes. "Does that mean I will not be fined?"

"It means there will be no court case at all," he said gently. "You are free to leave and," he delved under the desk, "here are the toys. Give them to your children with our best wishes."

"But I must pay for them . . ." She began to open her handbag.

"No," he said. "We've something else for you."

He pushed an envelope across the desk and it bore her name.

She regarded it solemnly and glanced at me. "Open it," I said.

She did, and inside were fifty £1 notes.

"Money . . . ?" she said.

"We had a collection among all the policemen here," said the inspector. "We paid for your toys. There's about two hundred of us and every man has given five shillings, so there's money for future presents for your family. We want you to put this money into a post-office account, and use it only for Christmas and birthday presents. You'll get a little bit of interest on the money and I know P.C. Rhea will help you to open the account. So your twins will always have presents like other children . . ."

Julia was sobbing as she clutched the money to her thin chest and I put an arm about her. I felt my own eyes grow moist and I know the inspector was feeling very emotional about it. Julia didn't know what to say so I suggested she write a letter to thank them when she returned home. There was no fuss about it, no formal presentation, no publicity, just a show of genuine affection and understanding from two hundred policemen towards one girl who'd been badly treated by a man.

* * *

Later, my own family was about to increase. Our fourth child was almost due and I knew that in the very near future I would have to drive Mary to the Maternity Home near Malton. I didn't want a last-minute panic like the previous occasion and, sure enough, the warning signals began late one evening. I rang the hospital and they accepted her; within half an hour, Mary was in my car and we were driving swiftly but carefully across the valley to the country-based maternity home. A neighbour had come into care for the other children.

We left it closer than I'd realised. Mary said the contractions were beginning and I realised that a birth was imminent so it was with infinite relief that I reached the hospital in time. The sister suggested I wait, for surely I would be a dad yet again within a very short time.

I entered the plain waiting-room full of old magazines and hard chairs and found another young man sitting there waiting. He was clearly a farm labourer, having come straight from some smelly job in his old clothes. He sat on one of the chairs, twisting a flat cap in his powerful hands and gazing at the floor. He smiled briefly as I entered and I settled down opposite; I felt very much the experienced dad with a score of three to my credit so far.

I greeted the young fellow with "Now then" as we do in Yorkshire and he nodded a brief response, all the time wringing his cap.

"It's not like a sow, is it?" he suddenly spoke.

"Er, no, I suppose not," I responded to his odd statement.

"Sows eat theirs, eh? If you don't do summat quickly, they eat their young. Cats do an' all," he commented.

"Humans aren't like that," I said by way of saying something constructive and helpful.

"My first." He squeezed the hat until I felt it must fall apart in those massive hands.

"My fourth." I felt a glow of parental pride as I realised we'd not eaten any of ours.

"It's not like horses either, is it?" he resumed after a break in our conversation.

"Horses?" I puzzled.

"Aye, foaling. Horses foaling. They've got to get ropes on the feet and drag 'em out. I've done it many a time . . . nasty business. This won't be like that, will it?"

"No, it won't," I assured him, feeling it wise to refrain from explaining that some human births weren't all that easy.

There followed a long period of silence, during which he mangled his cap until it looked like a battered dish-cloth. Then he smiled and said:

"It'll not be like cows either, will it?"

"Cows?" I must have sounded baffled by this time.

"Cows roll on their calves sometimes. Big hefty cows, lashing about. They roll over and smother their calves if you're not there . . ."

"The nurses will look after ours," I assured him, wondering about the size of his wife.

He smiled at my blithe reassurance and settled down, then suddenly paced the floor and put the mangled hat on his untidy hair. He stopped right in front of me and peered at me seriously.

196

"It's not like lambs, is it?" he asked, those anxious eyes boring into mine.

"Lambs?" I shook my head.

"If the mother dies, they give the lamb to another ewe; they skin a dead lamb and hide the smell and put the skin over the orphan . . ."

I visualised mothers wearing wigs to confuse babies; I visualised babies being painted with some fluid to disguise their smells so that foster-mothers would accept them . . .

"It's not a bit like that," I said, and he returned to his chair where he recommenced his wringing motions.

We waited another five minutes and he smiled at me.

"I'm glad we're not like cuckoos," he winked. "Crafty old birds, those, eh? Laying their eggs in another nest and letting somebody else feed them and bring them up . . ."

"I think a lot of humans are just a bit like that," I laughed with him.

The sister came through and addressed him. "Mr Winford?"

"Aye?" he leapt to his feet and clapped the mangled cap on his head once again.

"You've got a son," she smiled. "And he and his mother are both well."

"I reckon he'll be a thoroughbred sire like his dad," and he followed the nurse with gleeful pride in his eyes.

I waited, musing over his curious view of natural birth, and within half an hour the sister called me in.

"A daughter, Mr Rhea," she announced. "And both are fine."

For some reason, I thought of a fawn.

**THE END**

## ALSO BY NICHOLAS RHEA

Don't miss a book in the series — join our mailing list:

www.joffebooks.com

Thank you for reading this book. If you enjoyed it please leave feedback on Amazon or Goodreads, and if there is anything we missed or you have a question about, then please get in touch. The author and publishing team appreciate your feedback and time reading this book.

We're very grateful to eagle-eyed readers who take the time to contact us. Please send any errors you find to corrections@joffebooks.com

Printed in Great Britain
by Amazon

38980839R00121